"JIM SILVER
IS IN THE ALKALI DESERT!"

"Silver?" repeated Yates stupidly. "Jim Silver—down here?"

He looked half-witted as he spoke. His mouth opened. He stepped forward a little, exactly like a man who has received a heavy blow that has half-benumbed him.

"Silver is down here, somewhere in the desert. My men have seen his wolf. That means that I shall see Silver, before long."

"Well then, we'll smash him when he comes! How many are with him?"

"He seems to be alone. But he's enough, by himself. Pull yourself together, and try to start your brain working. I say that Jim Silver is somewhere near this town!"

Books by Max Brand

Published by POCKET BOOKS

Max Brand

VALLEY OF
VANISHING MEN

PUBLISHED BY POCKET BOOKS NEW YORK

POCKET BOOKS, a Simon & Schuster division of
GULF & WESTERN CORPORATION
1230 Avenue of the Americas, New York, N.Y. 10020

ISBN: 0-671-83310-3

First Pocket Books printing September, 1949

10   9   8   7   6

POCKET and colophon are trademarks of Simon and Schuster.

Printed in the U.S.A.

Contents

CHAPTER I

The Gray Wolf

IT WAS one of those gorges which seem to have been plowed through the mountains with some vast mechanical instrument that cuts with equal ease through hard and soft. Granite had yielded like butter to the edge of that imagined tool. And Trainor, looking up from the edge of the creek, could see the steep and polished cliffs rising on either hand, beyond the climbing of man or beast. At the top, there was an occasional fringing of trees, which leaned over the gorge as though peering curiously down into its depths.

But he had little time to look at the peculiarities of nature, because he was bound for Alkali Valley, in the desert, and his mind was preoccupied by that letter from the hotel keeper which had said, briefly:

Your brother left the hotel two weeks ago, intending to be gone not more than five days. We have heard no word from him. Travel in Alkali Valley, as you know, is dangerous. We think you should be informed of his continued absence.

That was why he had saddled his roan, left his job punching cows, and had hurried at once down the trails that led south. He had been nearly eight days on the way, and still that letter which was curled up in his breast pocket kept drifting into words through his mind. He had finally, on this day, submitted to the heat and was plugging along with his thoughts on the unknown

1

dangers of Alkali Valley, when he heard the unforgettable note of a wolf on a blood trail.

He had just turned a corner of the canyon and had gone past what men in the West call a "devil's slide"— a steep-sided heap of débris which was stacked up against the side wall of the valley and ran to the very top of the cliff, almost two hundred feet above. Now, looking back and up toward the cry of the wolf, he saw a mule deer running in the sky, as it were, with a great gray wolf in pursuit. They were so close to the edge of the precipice that the blue of the sky outlined their straining bodies.

Ordinarily, a mule deer could run away from the fastest wolf that ever walked on pads, but this stag had been laboring hard for a long time and was nearly spent. And the wolf ran as though it knew that the staggering strides of the deer must stop at any moment. A red rag of lolling tongue whipped from the side of the lobo's mouth. At that short distance, Trainor could almost see the green blood lust in the eye of the monster. For it seemed one of the freaks of its species—a creature that might weigh as much as one hundred and fifty pounds; a giant of its kind such as Westerners see once in a lifetime.

Trainor had no need of venison, but he hated cattle-killing wolves, those wise and long-headed murderers. That was why he pulled his Winchester out of the time-polished leather of its holster that ran down beside his leg. He balanced the gun—a bright sword flash of light in the sun—and tucked the butt into the hollow of his shoulder.

A moment later, a hard-nosed bullet would have clipped through the body of the gray wolf, but here the deer took things into its own charge. It had come to the end of its strength, and whirling suddenly, it stood at bay with head down, with hind legs sprawled wide, the quarters sinking toward the ground. It was the perfect picture of desperate and hopeless courage as it wheeled.

The gray wolf checked itself so abruptly that it skidded a bit on braced legs, and that was where chance took a hand for the mule deer. For the lobo, as it skidded, slued around to the side and slid off onto the top of that devil's slide.

Trainor grunted with horror, and dropped his rifle back into its holster, for it was a grim death that the lobo was falling toward. Nothing in the world could keep it from shooting down that crumbling, sharp-angled gravel heap into the waters of the creek—and those waters were running like galloping horses toward the white of the rapids just below. Out of those rapids gleamed the sharp teeth of polished rocks, ready to spear any living thing that entered the jaws of the cataract.

The gray wolf was using brains worthy of a king of its kind. Instead of turning and trying vainly to claw its way back up the treacherous slope, and thereby loosening under its feet a constantly increasing flood of almost liquid gravel, the lobo went down like a mountain sheep, head first, with braced legs. And as it saw a change in the surface to this side or that, the animal would jump for it. The new soil sometimes held for an instant, slowing the fall. It seemed to Trainor, as he stared, that the lobo might actually beat the law of gravitation, but a moment later the whole face of the bottom of the slope gave way with a rush and hurled the hunter down toward the stream.

Even then the wolf did not surrender to fate. Instead of trying to get into the shoal water on the nearer side of the creek—a thing which the impetus of its fall rendered impossible—the lobo actually ran with the running gravel and, from the bank of the creek, hurled itself far out into the air.

It was a glorious leap. It was like a javelin cast from the shore, and again Trainor believed, and earnestly hoped, that the brave beast would clear the speed of the central current and get into the slack of water on the farther side.

There was a fighting chance, for a brief space, as the lobo pointed its nose at a slight angle upstream, fighting against the sweep of the water as it worked in toward the farther shore. But then the central current gained upon the brave swimmer. Little by little the distance between the wolf and the shore widened. The main stream got hold and bore the lobo down, twisting it in circles of increasing rapidity.

Still it did not surrender, as most men or beasts would have done, to the inevitable. It struggled a bit to the side, where a rock point jutted out from the face of the stream, with a white bow wave spreading out from it on either side. And Trainor, with a gasp of admiration, saw the lobo reach with paws and teeth for that haven, that anchor point. No human brain could have tried better.

It was a useless effort. The descent of the wolf was stopped for one instant only. Then the creek waters, as though angered, rose in a wave that submerged the lobo. The next moment it was shooting down the stream again.

Still it fought, pointing nose upstream when the currents failed to start it whirling helplessly round and round.

Trainor, with a groan of sympathy, flung himself out of the saddle. There was a ten-foot branch of a dead tree that had fallen from the cliff top above onto the floor of the ravine. He snatched that up and ran hip-deep into the current. Farther he dared not go, for even at that depth the currents shook and staggered him, and the roar of the rapids took on a snarling sound that had a personal meaning for him.

Now, looking up the stream, he saw the wolf coming. Wild beasts avoid men even more than they avoid death, as a rule, but this big lobo, with ears pricking forward more sharply, with eyes bright with understanding, aimed itself straight at the branch that was thrust out toward it.

The heart of Trainor rose in his breast. He knew, that instant, that he would never again be able to set a trap or point a gun at a wolf. He could not slaughter any member of a tribe so wise and brave and steadfast. It would be murder, he felt.

Right down at the branch the wolf came. A freak of the twisting current brought it close in, almost in arm's reach of Trainor, and then a vagary of the same current whirled it away again beyond the tip of the branch. It was lost!

No, at the last minute, even while it was spinning in the current, the lobo managed to make a convulsive effort and catch the very end of the branch in its teeth.

The strain that followed almost pulled Trainor off his feet. For an instant, he heard the noise of the rapids like a death song swelling in his ears. Then he rebraced his feet, swayed his weight back, and found that he was just able to meet the pull of the flying water.

And the wolf, although only the tip of the nose and the eyes showed now and again, through the smother of the spray, kept its grip, was drawn in a little, and still a little more.

They were winning! Now Trainor could make a backward step into calmer and more shoaling water. Now he could bring the wolf after him into the shallows. And suddenly, touching bottom, with a great bound the gray lobo flung itself forward onto the shore.

What followed was far stranger than anything that had gone before. Nature should have asserted itself the instant that the wolf hit firm ground. It should have turned into a gray streak and disappeared at once among the boulders.

Instead, it first sent out a sparkling cloud of spray as

it shook the water from its coat. Then it sat down, pointed its nose toward the top of the cliff, and uttered a long, long howl.

Did it see the mule deer up yonder? Was it sending up a last call of hate and a promise of revenge toward the lucky bit of venison?

Trainor glanced toward the ridge and saw a thing that took his breath indeed. For a rider was up there, a big man sitting the saddle on a great stallion that shone like polished copper in the blaze of the sun. The wolf, the stallion, the rider, joined to make one symbol in the mind of Trainor.

"Silver!" he shouted. "Jim Silver!"

CHAPTER II

Alkali Valley

JIM SILVER waved his hand. His voice came dimly to the ears of Trainor, asking him to wait there, because Silver would come down to the floor of the ravine through a gap that opened a little distance ahead. Then he shouted: "Stay there, Frosty! Hi!"

The gray wolf dropped to the ground like a stone in answer to the gesture and the voice of the man. There he remained, while Silver disappeared along the top of the ridge.

"Frosty!" said Trainor, shaking his head with awe and admiration. "Frosty!"

The bright eyes of the wolf shifted toward him, but flashed instantly back to the point where his master had last appeared. Now that the sun began to dry his fur, he appeared a dust-gray, ideally fitted for melting into Western backgrounds of rocks and desert or sunburned grasses. His great paws seemed as large as the hands of a man. His head was like the head of a bear. He seemed too big to belong to his kind. And then a flood of tales came sweeping over the mind of Trainor, reminding him of the feats that were attributed to this huge beast—feats of almost human intelligence. Men said that Frosty, under the guidance of Jim Silver, was as valuable in war as three knife-bearing Apaches—that hardly a trail could be laid down that Frosty was unable to solve and follow at the will of Jim Silver.

Here the rider himself appeared around the next corner of the ravine.

At his call, Frosty leaped to his feet and went like a bullet to give greeting. He flung himself high at the side of Silver, bounding up again and again, biting at the hand of his master with terrible fangs that seemed able to sever the thick of the wrist joint.

That was the affectionate meeting of the pair, after danger had come between them, and Trainor laughed at the sight. It was something to remember. It was something to tell to his friends when he was back among them again. He had seen Silver and the wolf acting like happy children together. Now he could hear that savage snarling which was Frosty's nearest approach to a tone of caress. And now he could hear Silver laughing with pleasure.

The big fellow grew on the eye, and so did his horse. They seemed almost gigantic, in the eyes of Trainor, as Silver drew rein. But perhaps that was chiefly the effect of the excited imagination of Trainor, the effect of those accumulated legends which had been heaping up around the name of Silver and his horse and his wolf during these last years. Wherever men met together along the mountain desert, whether in logging camp or bunkhouse, or tramp jungle, or hotel veranda, there was sure to be talk of Silver before the long evening was over. If someone spoke of a feat of strength, Silver's name came up for comparison. If there was talk of a fast horse which had recently cleaned up the prizes at a rodeo, Parade had to be brought in for comparison. A cowpuncher would say: "As strong in the legs as Parade!" Or "Longer-winded than Parade!" Or "As fine an eye as Parade ever had in his head!"

For this was the way of establishing a superlative. And when the talk was of humans, then there was sure to be mention of gun or hand or wit that brought in again the name of the hero. That was why, when Trainor looked at this man, his heart swelled and enlarged to receive a noble idea. As Silver leaped down from the saddle and held out a hand, Trainor looked with a sort of worship into that handsome brown face.

But more than the bright, piercing eye, so strangely direct and steady, more than the big spread of forehead, Trainor was impressed by the sheer physical fitness of this man. He seemed ready to enter a race the next moment, or stand in the ring and fight for his life against great odds.

Well, one does not often see a fat panther! And Silver lived a life as natural, as rugged, as full of labor and effort as that of any wild beast that has to hunt for a living every day of its life. All spare flesh was worked away from his face, from his throat. His shirt was open, and over the arch of the breast bones, Trainor could see the ardent pull of the network of muscles. No wonder this man had endurance, on foot, like a running Indian. He had the depth of lungs for it, the slender hips, the wiry, powerful legs to give force for locomotion. And set on the top of this mechanism of grace and speed and endurance, there were the shoulders and the long, heavy arms of the man fit to heave and draw—and fight for his life!

Trainor, gripping that hand, smiled into the brown face of Silver and then laughed a little.

"Silver," he said, "I thought it was just an ordinary wolf, when I saw it up there running the deer. I was going to take a crack at it with my rifle. And then— well, then it took the slide!"

"Did you think that it was only an ordinary wolf?" asked Silver. "Then what made you risk your neck by wading into the creek to save it?"

"I wasn't risking my neck."

"I saw the water beat at you and curl up around your hips," said Silver calmly. "I saw the riffle of the current in your wake. It was hard for you to keep your feet, in there. And what made you do it for an ordinary, cattle-killing lobo?"

"Because he was fighting like a man, and a damn brave man."

Silver handled Trainor for one quick instant with his eyes and then he smiled a bit as though he were embarrassed by a personal compliment.

"Old Frosty!" he said, and the gray wolf growled at his hand and licked it. "It was a kind thing and a nervy thing that you did," went on Silver. "I'm thanking you, pardner. Which way does your trail lead?"

"Alkali," said Trainor, "if you've ever heard of that town."

"Alkali?" said Silver, with a bit of a start. "Why, that's queer. I'm going in that direction myself!"

He took off his hat and wiped his forehead with a handkerchief. Trainor saw with a curious excitement the spots of gray hair over the temples which, in the beginning, men said, had given a name to Silver. They looked like little horns just breaking through.

"We'll ride along together," said Silver, "if you don't mind. What takes you in that direction? Working in the mines?"

"No," said Trainor, "I'm working on a lost trail. My brother was down there and faded into the desert one day. He never came back, and I want to find out where he went."

"I've heard of other men," said Silver slowly, "who rode out of that town and vanished in Alkali Valley. That's why I'm heading in that direction."

"Silver," demanded Trainor suddenly, "are you going toward Alkali because you think that Barry Christian is around there?"

"I don't know," said Silver. "I'm only guessing. But we can ride together most of the way."

It was a happiness to Ben Trainor that made him squirm in the saddle and caused him to laugh a good deal, rather foolishly, all the distance that Silver rode beside him. After all, Ben Trainor had a good deal of boy in his make-up. It made most strangers take him and his cheerful, smiling face rather lightly, but that face could harden in a pinch as quickly as his hand could turn into a fist. Physically, he was neither large nor small, neither handsome nor ugly, but there was a spirit in the heart of Trainor that was a bright and ever-rising fountain.

They went out of the canyon into the gray sweep of Alkali Valley. A whirlwind promptly covered them with alkali dust that kept the horses sneezing for some time afterwards. Now they had to ride with their bandannas drawn over the bridges of their noses. Their eyes puckered and grew red of rim. Only Frosty seemed perfectly contented as he slunk before them over the gray sands, melting into the background the moment he was at any distance.

He was continually roving, shifting here and there, and continually lifting his nose to read any story that might come down the wind. Once or twice he put up a rabbit, and the second time, since the jack was big and looked fat, a gun jumped into Silver's hand, spoke, and disappeared, all in a single gesture. The rabbit dropped into a cactus scrub from its death leap, and Frosty brought it obediently to the master.

"That'll make supper," said Silver, as he cleaned the kill. "You're welcome to have it with me. Or do you have to go on into the town?" he asked, as they rode on again.

"I have to go on into the town," answered Trainor.

"Well, there you are," said Silver, pointing ahead.

All that Trainor could see, at first, was the wide sweep of the distant hills, rolling low, like heat clouds against the horizon. And he saw the Spanish bayonet here and there, and grisly cactus forms, and the nightmare shape of the ocotillo, and whatever barbed spikes and noisome varnishes could preserve from the teeth of deer or desert cattle. Finally, he saw a winking light in the distance and knew it was the sun flashing from glass. That was Alkali town, far away.

"There you are," said Silver, "but my trail goes this way. If you have to hunt long and hard for your brother, we may meet again. Do you mind a bit of advice?"

"No," said Trainor. "I'd like to have it—from you."

"Do a lot of looking and very little talking in Alkali," said Silver. "That's my advice. Sometimes things will show themselves, if a man waits long enough."

He gripped the hand of Trainor and said, with a faint smile:

"Frosty will remember you. So shall I!"

Then he rode away, letting Parade stretch out into a swinging canter that bore him off so rapidly that Trainor could see how much the gait of his mustang had held Silver back this day.

Where would the man go, if not into the town itself? All that he needed, men said, were salt and a gun; he would find enough to eat with that provision and no other. Therefore, at what dry camps would he halt, what trails would he pick up and use the nose of Frosty for following?

Trainor jogged his horse steadily on until he came into a beaten trail, and this led him rapidly to a road, deeply rutted by freight wagons. This, in turn, carried him to Alkali.

It was just one of those unpainted towns, half of frame and half of canvas, which look so time-dried that the wind might pick them up and scatter them over the desert the next time a storm blew. But Trainor knew that fortunes had passed through that town from the mines that were dug into the slopes of the southern hills. The mines had been failing for a long time, now, and Alkali was shriveling rapidly, but a sense of an exciting past breathed to him out of the old shacks as he went by.

Then he saw the Wilbur Hotel, tied his horse at the hitch rack, and went over the creaking boards of the veranda into the dark coolness of the lobby.

He said to the one-armed clerk at the desk: "My name is Trainor, and—"

"Wait a minute," interrupted the clerk.

He disappeared into another room and came back with a tall, lean, pale-faced man whose hair had disappeared from the crown of his head.

"You're Ben Trainor?" he asked. "My name is Wilbur." He paused to consider Trainor. "I'll show you your brother's stuff," he added, and led the way up two flights of noisy stairs to an attic. There he pulled a tarpaulin-wrapped bundle from among a mass of trunks and suit-cases and dropped the burden on the floor.

"Maybe you can find out something from this stuff," said Wilbur. "Otherwise—well, there's the desert, and it doesn't answer many questions."

"While my brother was here," said Trainor, "did you see him about with any suspicious characters? Notice anything about what he did?"

"Most of the characters in Alkali are suspicious," said Wilbur. "That's why I charge high prices in this hotel. This is one of the ends of the trail, Mr. Trainor. If you want to look that stuff over, I'll show you to a room."

He took Trainor down to the floor below and opened for him a small bedroom.

"You had something in your mind when you wrote me the letter. There was something between the lines," insisted Trainor.

Wilbur looked out of the window as a wall of desert dust went by and allowed the face of the saloon across the street to be seen again.

"I had an idea," he said at last, "but ideas are cheap."

"I'd like to hear this one," answered Trainor.

"Well, then," said Wilbur, "my idea was, after he was a week overdue, that he would never come back. I'm sorry to say that, and I hope there's nothing in it. I've had the same ideas about other people, though, and I'm generally right."

"What made you think that?" asked Trainor, tense with fear and excitement.

"I don't know," said Wilbur. "Your brother Clive was just a little too well-washed for this part of the world. He kept the salt washed out of his shirt, and that's being almost a dandy down here in Alkali."

He turned, then, and left the room.

CHAPTER III

The Knife

TRAINOR uncorded that bundle, flung open the flaps, and smelled the staleness of the clothes. A well-battered pair of knee boots, a canvas coat, some torn shirts, socks, and other odds and ends of clothes made up the bulk of the package. A canvas-backed note-book in one pocket of the coat and a shard of brittle, black rock in the other side pocket completed the list.

To that bit of stone, Trainor paid no attention. The note-book was a different matter, for he knew his brother's habit of writing down casual and important details in the pages of a book from day to day.

There were six months' notes in the thirty filled pages of the book. Half of the items were unintelligible scribblings, aids to the memory. And Ben Trainor got forward to the last bits, which must have been written closest to the time of Clive's departure from Alkali. Everything was very broken and haphazard. Clive was no romantic lady's man, but he mentioned a girl a number of times.

The references ran like this, at different times:

"Where she has nothing to gain, why shouldn't a woman be trusted?"

Later: "She's not pretty enough to be crooked."

Then: "It's money that she's after, and I'm a fool."

Finally: "Well, it's better to be a fool about a woman once than never to be a fool at all."

That was all Ben Trainor found to suggest that a woman had something to do with the disappearance of his brother. He thought that the references were so strong, considering the cold-blooded nature of Clive so far as girls were concerned, that once he was able to spot the girl, he would be able to find out exactly why and where Clive had gone from the town.

He returned to the study of the note-book again. But there was not a single other phrase that caught his attention except this, just two pages before the end: "Gold should not be wrapped up in anything so black."

That made Ben Trainor look at the little splinter of black rock that he had taken out of the pocket of the canvas coat. He broke it in two and could see no glint of yellow. He broke it again, and this time he distinctly saw the glitter of a very fine yellow beading.

His teeth gripped hard together. His scalp prickled and contracted, for he knew that the two greatest themes of misery had been sounded by his brother before disappearing: woman and gold!

There was an assay office in the town, of course. He got out of the hotel at once, merely pausing in the lobby to say to Wilbur that he could dispose of Clive's old clothes as he saw fit. He, Ben Trainor, had no more use for them.

Wilbur looked him over with that half-cold and half-sardonic eye before he answered: "You've found the same trail, Trainor. I suppose the same desert will be swallowing you, one of these days. It has a stomach that likes red meat, they say."

But Trainor overlooked that remark and went straight down the street to the first assay office. In a sense it was a court of final appeal and of grim judgment. He saw a bearded man of sixty coming out of the door laughing and prancing like a colt. He saw inside, a big, grim man who kept staring fixedly at a scrap of paper and shaking his head at it. The blue around the eyes and the white about the mouth of the miner told how frightfully he had suffered to get his specimen for the assay office, and now the paper was telling him, calmly, in words and figures that could not be doubted, that his specimen from the mine was worthless.

There was a short receiving counter, and behind it a man with a gray head, a fine brow, the tired face of a scholar who bends too much over his books at night. A red-headed lad sitting in a corner made a fine contrast with the man in charge. The boy was apparently there for the sake of doing odd jobs, and now he rested as only a boy can rest, his whole body slumped into a lump and his eyes blank with daydreams.

To the elderly clerk, Trainor gave the specimen and

saw it wrapped up, ticketed, labeled, his name taken for references. He could have the report the next day, he was told.

But as he listened, Trainor kept staring at the hands of the other instead of at his face. For those hands had trembled strangely, had been noticeably nervous and unsure as they made the package. Trainor glanced suddenly up and saw a slight but distinct compression about the lips of the clerk.

Then he turned away, puzzled, troubled.

He could be sure that the sight of that very tiny shard of stone had made a great impression on the clerk of the assay office. It had made such an impression that the man had had the look of one about to cry out loud with astonishment and excitement.

Trainor went through the door to the sidewalk. Down the street there was a crowd pouring along with the elderly man who had apparently just received a good report from the assay office, and he was still flinging up his hands and heels like a young fool.

There was great desire in Trainor to be alone because he had small bits of things that he wanted to put together—those notes in the book of his lost brother, the warnings of Wilbur, the odd actions of the clerk of the assay office. So he turned down a side alley into the next street of the town and saw, immediately before him, the hurrying, chunky form of the same red-headed lad he had seen in the assay office.

Something clicked, like a closing trap, in the mind of Trainor. He drew a deduction, a relationship, he hardly knew why, between the nervous hands of the assay clerk and this scurrying messenger. For he could see the white envelope of a letter in the hand of the boy.

A moment before, there had been no pressing message to be sent from the office. But since Trainor's coming, it had become necessary to rush the boy right away.

Ben Trainor followed, lengthening his stride, until he saw the youngster duck up an obscure alley between two buildings. When he came to that alley in turn, he saw the boy knocking at the back door of a building which must front on the main street, a building with a false front that rose in a triangle half a story above the rest of the structure.

Trainor did not follow, directly. Instead, he crossed the mouth of the alley and walked on, turned after a moment, retraced his steps across the alley slowly, again. This time he saw the rear door opening, and a black-coated man with a wide black hat on his head taking the letter from the boy—a man whose face seemed very pale, perhaps by contrast with the darkness of his hat and coat, a young and handsome fellow whose pallor might be that of sickness or of too much night life.

Trainor went on, still more slowly.

The get-up of the fellow in the black coat was exactly that which a professional gambler would be apt to use. They could generally be spotted by a garb which they all seemed to think was merely that of a man of money and plenty of idle time on his hands.

Very well, then, thought Trainor, as he came back into the main street of Alkali, there was some connection between the assay office and a gambler at a back door—of what?

It was not hard to spot the building that he wanted from its high, pyramidal false front. It was the saloon which carried the name, "Golden Hope."

In the Golden Hope there was a tall young fellow with a pale and handsome face who had to do with letters received from the assay office. And that was to Trainor very interesting indeed.

He sauntered on down the street, trying to make something more of this queer bit of evidence. He passed the shack which carried a small legend across one window:

"John Mahan, Deputy Sheriff," and as he saw it, he was greatly tempted to walk straight into the place and lay his cards on the table before the man of the law.

That would be dangerous. What he knew was perhaps best locked up in his breast. A story told to one man is told practically to the entire world.

He went up the street again and entered the bar of the Golden Hope. It was a long bar that ran down a side of a narrow room. Doors opened at the back and in the opposite wall. Apparently it was quite an establishment, and the three bartenders on duty told that a big crowd was expected as the usual patronage. There were only a dozen drinkers now, leaning their elbows at the bar and taking whisky or beer, and Trainor got a place at one corner of the bar and ordered a beer.

It was flat stuff, without much head, but he accepted it without a complaint. As he sipped it, he glanced over the men in the place and thought that he never had seen a harder lot.

True, nearly all of the men in Alkali were a rough crew. Unshaven fellows in battered or even tattered clothes are apt to look fairly grim, but the three bartenders, particularly one with a twisted face, were special choices in the way of evil. Even the men who leaned at the bar had the look of hangers-on rather than of regular miners out of work or blowing in their pay. There was no gaiety about them. There was no sense of revel. All voices were lowered in this saloon, and Trainor could not help feeling that speculative, curious eyes were turned toward him now and again.

What caught his attention next, with a start, was a knife with which a man seated at one of the little round tables in a corner was aimlessly whittling at a stick, dropping the shavings in fine curls into a spittoon. For the handle of that knife, as much as Trainer could see of it, seemed to be composed of gray pearl and black.

And exactly such a knife had belonged to his lost brother!

He could feel a cold sweat starting on his forehead; he could feel the skin of his brow gathering and prickling. So he stared down into his glass of beer, sipped it, called up again in his mind the detailed picture of the fellow with the knife.

He was a broad, formidable chunk of a man, with a great double-tufted black mustache that bristled when the whittler compressed his lips. This he did very often, for he seemed to have a habit of frowning and scowling at the same instant, during his meditations.

Perhaps he was thinking at that very moment of the last struggle of Clive Trainor!

Vainly Ben Trainor tried to tell himself that the knife probably meant nothing, that there were sure to be thousands of knives of pearl and black exactly like the one his brother had owned.

But he knew it was not true. Black horn and clean gray pearl had been overlaid on the handle of Clive's knife. And there was one nick rather deep, and close to the end—a nick in the pearl.

At this moment the man of the black mustache laid down the knife. That temptation was too much for Ben Trainor. He crossed the floor with a casual step, picked up one of a pile of newspapers that lay on another table, and at the same time looked intently at the fully exposed knife.

Toward one end of it, there was a nick that ran into the pearl and showed yellow metal of the frame of the handle!

CHAPTER IV

The Fighter

PASSION was strong in young Ben Trainor, and it almost mastered him now. The tide of it made him want to drive straight at the fellow of the black mustache. Then he remembered that, like a fool, he had not brought a gun. For that matter, he was no expert with a revolver. He could shoot his share of meat with a rifle, but a revolver, in his life of work, was an almost useless adornment. And such fellows as this one of the mustache were fairly sure to be experts. He had the look of a fighter. The long scar that jagged down a side of his cheek was the sort of a thing that a knife stroke might have registered.

Besides, there were other ways of getting hold of a knife than by murdering the owner.

He stepped to the next table, saying:

"Pardon me, stranger. That's a good-looking knife you have there."

The fellow was smoothing absently, with the tips of his fingers, the stick which he had been whittling. Now he looked up rather askance at Trainor, and the turn of his head brought out the bulging strength of his neck tendons.

"Yeah," he said. "It's a pretty good knife."

His paw gathered the knife, his thumb clicked the blade shut, and he dropped it into his pocket. There was profound insolence in the action, as though to stop with it any further talk on the subject. And the suspicions of Trainor burned up to a white heat.

"Can a fellow buy knives like that in this town?" he asked, controlling his voice.

"Yeah, if you know which pawnshop to try in," said the other.

He stood up from his chair and looked Trainor up and down. Then he turned his back to stride away toward the bar.

"Wait a minute," said Trainor, touching his shoulder.

That shoulder was hard-padded with muscles. The chunky man spun around at the touch.

"Yeah? Yeah?" he queried angrily. "What's the matter now? Wanta know something more? Wanta find out where you can buy some soap and give yourself a clean start?"

Two or three of those idlers at the bar began to laugh loudly.

"Wake him up, Blacky," said one of them.

And that bartender with the twisted face was smiling —on one side only.

"You're talking pretty hard talk, partner," said Trainor.

"If I was your partner," the man called Blacky said, "I'd change my job and get a new kind." And he opened his mouth and laughed in Trainor's face.

It was a great deal too much. The hand of Trainor moved like a flash beyond his control. The flat of it struck fairly across the open mouth of Blacky.

"Hi!" yelled two or three voices at the bar. "Let him have it, Blacky!"

Blacky had accepted the blow and stopped laughing. He was smiling now, instead. And then, putting up his guard, he moved in at Trainor with little dancing steps, the left fist jerking out in feints at the head, the right hand poised for serious business. He had his jaw tucked down behind the shelter of his massive left shoulder, and Trainor knew that he had on his hands an artist in fisticuffs.

Well, Trainor was no such artist, but he could stand blows and give them. He tried the effect of a hearty right swing for the head followed by a smashing straight left. Blacky blocked the first, ducked the second, and as he straightened, exploded a punch on the chin of Trainor that dropped him into a deep well of darkness.

He wakened with an acrid smell of dust in his nostrils, and found himself lying on his face in the street. They had flung him out there like a dog, and inside the saloon he could hear the noisy, laughing, cheerful voices.

He turned, ready to plunge in through the swing doors and fight to a finish. But he checked himself before he had taken a step, for a tall, sallow man who leaned against a hitch post near by was saying:

"It's no good, kid. They've got you licked once. Why give 'em a chance to lick you a second time?"

The advice was good and true, and Trainor walked slowly down that street, rubbing the sore lump that was rising on his jaw.

These men of Alkali were hard. They were very hard. They were too much, perhaps, for a fellow of his caliber to compete against. Mere strength of nerve and hand would not turn the trick against them. Instead, there would have to be brain work, and perhaps the power of the law would help.

He went to the office of John Mahan, the deputy sheriff.

John Mahan was a little man with a big chest and a big head. He was standing, now, saying to one of those black-coated fellows of the gambling ilk:

"And if I go down there and start looking over your roulette wheel, I'm going to look deeper than the floor. I'm going to root up the whole damn place. I've heard too much talk about you, and if I hear any more, you're going to get news from me that'll scorch you up. Now get out of here and get good."

The other man went out with a sick smile that was intended for defiance. Mahan turned to Trainor and demanded:

"Now, what's eating you?"

"I've just swallowed a punch on the chin," said Trainor calmly, "but that's not why I'm here."

"Just in to pass the time of day?" asked the aggressive deputy. "Is that it?"

"My name is Benjamin Trainor," he answered. "I have a brother named Clive Trainor. He left this town more than three weeks ago intending to be gone only a few days. He went into the desert and he hasn't come back."

"Sorry," said the deputy sheriff. "Who went with him?"

"I don't know."

"Well," said Mahan impatiently, "what do you want me to do about it?"

Anger flushed the face of Trainor.

"I want you to listen to what I have to say without jumping me at every second word," he exclaimed.

Mahan looked him over calmly.

"All right, all right," he said, with a gesture. "I'll listen. But I can't listen long. This job of mine ain't a sitting-and-listening job. It's an up-and-doing job. Go ahead."

"Back there in the Golden Hope saloon," said Trainor, "I saw a fellow with a bushy pair of black mustaches—short, heavy chunk of a man—and he was whittling a stick with my brother's knife. Blacky, they called him."

"Blacky?" said the deputy sheriff. Then he pursed his lips and whistled.

"I tried to find out where he got that knife, and I collected a punch on the chin instead."

"Blacky's been in the ring," said the sheriff.

"I picked myself out of the street and came down here to see what the law will say about things."

"The law says that Blacky is a tough hombre," said

Mahan. "It says that he has some tough backing behind him. But the law says that if it can get a grip on Blacky, it'll sure put him behind the bars. Where do you hang out?"

"At Wilbur's Hotel."

"Go back there and wait. I'll try to get some news for you. Maybe I'll get Blacky while I'm getting the news."

CHAPTER V

Gun Play

TRAINOR returned to the Wilbur Hotel and went up to his room. His head was aching badly, so he lay down on his cot and closed his eyes and tried to forget the shooting pains that kept stabbing upward from the base of his brain. Presently, as any good cowpuncher will, he fell asleep. When he wakened, the room was filled with the swirling dusk of twilight and there was a heavy knocking at his door. He opened it on the heavy shoulders and the great head of John Mahan.

"Light a lamp," directed Mahan. "I've got some news, and it's all bad."

Trainor lighted a lamp on the center table and sat down to smoke a cigarette. The deputy sheriff walked impatiently up and down the room.

"I saw Blacky and I saw him just as he was throwing a leg over a horse, ready to get out of town," said Mahan. "I made him show me the knife. He swore that he got it from Cleveland's pawnshop. I made him come with me to the pawnshop. Cleveland is an old gray rat, and nobody can read his mind. When I asked him about the knife, he said it was right—Blacky had seen it in the window and bought it. I asked what the price was, and

Blacky answered up out of his turn. He said that he paid only seventy-five cents for that knife, because there was a nick in the pearl. Well, that was straight enough and likely enough, because I could see the nick. Then I asked Cleveland where he got that knife in the first place, but he couldn't say. All he knew was that he had bought it, one day, along with a lot of other stuff, and he couldn't remember the looks of the man who had sold it. That closed up that trail—tight."

Said Trainor, as his head cleared more and more: "Could Blacky have tipped a wink to Cleveland when he came into the shop with you?"

"I think there was something between them," answered the deputy sheriff. "Not because they looked at each other, but because they *didn't* look. I never saw their eyes crossing. Now, Trainor, have you any more stuff to tell me?"

"Out of my brother's canvas coat—he'd left it behind at the hotel—I found a note-book that had some remarks that seemed to tie up a girl and gold."

"Yeah, lots of girls and gold go together—or the girls don't go at all," remarked the other.

Trainor went on steadily: "And in another pocket of the same coat I found a bit of soft black stone. When I broke it open, I could see bits of gold glinting. I took that stone to the assay office. The clerk seemed a bit excited when he saw the specimen. He was so excited that he couldn't iron all the wrinkles out of his face. After I got out of the office, I saw a red-headed kid from the assayer's hoofing down the street. I thought it was a little queer that there was a message for the kid to run right out after I'd been in there. I followed and saw him give the letter in at the back door of the Golden Hope saloon. It was taken by a tall, youngish fellow, good-looking, with a pale face, long black coat, and a wide hat."

"Yates?" exclaimed John Mahan sharply. "You mean Doc Yates?"

"Perhaps that's his name. I don't know," said Trainor.

The deputy sheriff had stopped walking up and down. He stood still, staring out of very wide eyes. There was no doubt that he was a courageous chunk of a man. There was also no doubting that he was very frightened now.

He got out a plug of chewing tobacco, sank his teeth in a gnawed corner of it, and worked out a large bite which he stuck in the center of one cheek. It left a white spot on the outside. Still he rolled his eyes a bit from the window to the door as he began the mastication of that tobacco.

He went to the window, spat into the air, and turned back into the room.

"Listen, hombre," he said. "When I went to the window, just then, I went into danger. You know why?"

"No," said Trainor.

"Because there might be one of Yates's men across the street with a gun. Trainor, I'm here in Alkali trying to do a damned hard job. I'm trimming off the corners and making things hot for a lot of the crooks. But I'll tell you this: Doc Yates is a bigger man than I am in Alkali. He always has been and he always will be, as long as he wants to own the town. If you've got him against you— well, I advise you to roll your pack and get out of here. Get wherever you please, but get!"

"Wait a minute," pleaded Trainor. "There's a lot I want to know and—"

Mahan took him by the arm as he went on:

"The less questions you ask, the more you're likely to know. Cut me out a regular job, a man-sized job, and I'll try to do my duty. But don't ask me to tackle Doc Yates. Not till I've got a wiser brain in my head, and more people behind me."

"Leave Yates out of it, then," said Trainor. "I told you

my brother left this town more than three weeks ago. Is there any way of finding out whether or not Blacky left at the same time?"

"He's one of Yates's men. Maybe Yates will tell you," snapped the deputy sheriff, and left the room suddenly, with a mere wave of the hand by way of farewell.

Trainor washed, shaved, and went down to eat at a lunch counter around the corner. He hardly knew what he put in his mouth, his brain was so troubled, but there was one great and clear certainty. He had come to a place where the law would not follow him with its assistance. Deputy Sheriff Mahan could be counted out of the tangles that might ensue from the stay of Trainor in this town.

He paid his bill, left the smoke of the lunch counter, and stepped onto the street. The Best Bet saloon twinkled its lights at him across the way, and he went into it.

The beer was better here. He was vaguely aware that three men had come in behind him and lined up at the bar, but he paid little heed to them. His mind was too filled with his own problem.

He made a fool of himself from the first. He could see that. In the first place, by taking the ore to the assay office, he had obviously tipped his hand. In the second place, when he recognized the knife of his brother, he had been an idiot to ask direct questions of Blacky. In the third place, by going straight to the deputy sheriff, he had established in the minds of his enemies, whoever they might be, that he was on the trail of his missing brother.

What he had learned was that Doc Yates might be mixed up in this matter somewhere, and that Yates had behind him an organization so powerful that even the appointed officers of the law feared to touch him. All he had gained was the information that Blacky was probably mixed up in the disappearance of Clive Trainor. He could not even be sure of this. The pawnbroker might have told the honest truth about the sale of the knife.

In any case, it was certain that there had been some human agency that had to do with the disappearance of Clive. It was not merely a matter of the devouring desert. Whoever carried that knife to the pawnbroker's office—if Blacky were telling the truth—was the man that he wanted to see.

Yet Trainor felt certain that the deputy sheriff had given him the best possible advice, which was for him to get out of Alkali as fast as he could, while the getting was still in his power. He played in a game where the cards were stacked against him, where numbers were great odds in favor of the enemy, and where even the law could not assist him.

Yet he knew, as he sipped his beer, that he could not leave the town like a frightened dog. If his brother had been murdered, the same agents would have to put a knife into his own flesh.

He looked up from his reflections as angry voices suddenly began snarling—a typical saloon brawl. Two of the trio who had come in behind him were the trouble makers. One of them was a sad-faced cowpuncher, rather lean and bent of shoulders, the sort of a fellow in whom one could almost see the broken bones of many a fall from bucking horses, with the strength burned from all except his eyes. The other was a magnificent, tall man, a glorious body with a very small head set between the shoulders. He was almost an albino. His hair was silver-white; his brows were the same; his eyes were nearly colorless. It was like looking at the head of a statue. Something human and necessary seemed to be missing from it.

The bartender was reaching across the bar, pleading to the big man:

"Quit it, Josh! Quit it, will you? Dave Cormack didn't mean anything. He didn't say anything!"

"You lie!" shouted big Josh. "And *he* lies!"

"I what?" asked Dave Cormack, drawing back a little from the bar.

There was a sudden trampling and thundering of feet as the dozen other men at the bar rushed back against the opposite wall to get out of the bullet path. But Trainor stood with his beer, stunned, still only half removed from the world of his thoughts.

"Boys, don't start anything!" yelled the bartender. "Dave, step up here and have a drink on the house. Everybody have a drink. Josh May, have some sense, will you? Dave didn't mean nothing! He didn't say nothing!"

"You lie!" said Josh May. There was color in his eyes now. It was the yellow of flame. "Dave Cormack is a dirty sneak and a crooked—"

"Take this, then!" snarled Cormack softly, and flashed a gun.

There was a weapon in the hand of May, also. But as he pulled it, his flaring eyes found not Cormack, but Trainor in his place a little down the bar. And in the darting of that instant, Trainor understood that this quarrel was only a bluff, a pretense, and out of the roar of the guns would come only one result—the killing of an innocent bystander, whose name would be Benjamin Trainor!

His grip had hardened, at the same time, on the cold round of the beer glass. It was his only weapon. Even if he had a gun, there was not the slightest time for him to make a draw. That flash of May's eye made him act, and his action was to hurl the beer glass straight into the face of Josh May.

At the same time, his hat jumped off his head. The roar of the Colt thundered in his ears. He saw Josh May go a step backward with a yell of fear, throwing the gun away, clapping both hands to his face.

"Hey!" shouted Cormack. "Who asked strangers into this here man's fight?"

He swung, as he shouted, straight around toward Trainor. If one of the pair had failed to get the stranger, the other one would do his best. This time, Trainor had nothing but empty hands. He smashed out with all his might and saw the head of Cormack jerk far back. The bullet from his gun drove through the ceiling. The next moment the Colt was in the grasp of Trainor, covering his man.

Josh May, at a little distance, took advantage of the fact that the stranger was not pointing a weapon toward him. He leaped for the rear door of the room, and dived through it into thick obscurity. But Trainor marched Dave Cormack back onto the street while the bartender still loudly begged everybody to be friends, and swore that the house wanted to buy drinks all around.

Out in the street, Trainor pushed Dave Cormack into the black mouth of an alley and against a wall.

"Now, rat-face," said Trainor, "who was going to pay you for this job?"

"Do I get back the gun if I talk?" asked Cormack.

"Not much."

"Then you'll not get anything from me."

Trainor punched him again on the chin and heard the back of Cormack's head crack up against the wall. With the palm of his left hand he pushed the gunman back, holding up part of his weight until the wits of Cormack steadied again.

"That's only a starter," said Trainor. "There's nothing that I like better than beating up crooks. It's the only thing I'm fond of. Are you talking, Cormack? Who was to pay you for this job?"

"I'll talk, Trainor," said Cormack, "only give me back that gun afterward. You can unload it and everything. It don't mean nothing to you—only lemme have it back, will you?"

"I've asked you a question," said Trainor. "Now I'm going to knock your teeth down your throat."

"All right," answered Cormack wearily. "I'll tell you then. Doc Yates was going to pay us."

"How much?"

"Fifteen hundred bucks."

"To split three ways?"

"Yes."

"That's a lot of money for one man's killing," said Trainor. "Why does Doc Yates want me out of the way?"

"I dunno," said Cormack.

"What marching orders did you get?"

"To bump you off, and then turn your pockets inside out and bring Doc what you've got on you."

"Is that all?"

"Yeah, that's all."

"I ought to send you down the street to the deputy sheriff's office, but he's another rat—afraid to touch Yates. Yates knows it, and you know it. Am I right?"

"You're right," agreed Cormack. "I—I wish I'd never seen your mug."

"Get out of my sight then," commanded Trainor.

"Wait a minute," pleaded Cormack desperately. "That old gun doesn't mean anything to you, brother. I've got the price here for you to buy ten better guns. But it's broke in to my hand. It knows me, and I know it. I know just the amount it shoots crooked. Lemme have that gun, Trainor, will you, like a good fellow?"

Trainor laughed a little.

"If I could, I'd hang you up by the neck," he said. "The way it is, all I'm going to do is to turn you loose—like the fool I am—and keep your gun."

Cormack retreated, with a sidling step, to the mouth of the alley. There he turned, and snarled over his shoulder:

"If you have it in the morning, you'll have it dead!"

Then he vanished.

CHAPTER VI

The Girl

TRAINOR went straight back to the Wilbur Hotel. He only stopped under a ray of light that leaked through a half-opened shutter in order to examine the gun in which Cormack took such an interest. It was a single-shot Colt of an old make. The trigger was gone. The sights were gone. It was to be fired by flicking back the hammer with a touch of the thumb, and the slightest pressure raised that well-oiled, lightly set hammer. No doubt, to Cormack, this weapon represented more than the right hand of his best friend. Without that old instrument of murder, he would feel naked and helpless in this world.

After the examination, Trainor put the weapon into his clothes and went on toward the hotel, stepping lightly, rapidly, turning his head constantly. For he had a feeling that at any moment a form might step out from a doorway with the glimmer of steel in its hand.

When he reached the hotel, the lobby was empty except for Wilbur himself, who rose out of a chair and pointed toward a bundle.

"Trainor," he said, "there's no charge for your use of the room. I've got to ask you to step on. There's your bundle made up for you, and everything in it."

"You're turning me out of the place?" asked Trainor.

Wilbur shook his head. "It's no good. I'm sorry, but I can't keep you," he declared.

"You, too?" asked Trainor. "You're afraid of Doc Yates?"

The lips of Wilbur pinched together, but he nodded. Then he said: "Why be a fool, Trainor? You've shown plenty of nerve. You've made your try, and a large chunk of this town knows about what you've done. But why not get out of the place now and try to live out your life? We're all dead soon enough, anyway."

Trainor picked up the bundle and slung it over his right shoulder.

"I thought you were a man, Wilbur," he said, sneering.

"Not that much of a man," answered the hotel keeper. "In a town like this, there's only room for one man. You ought to be able to see that by this time."

Trainor went out to the stable behind the hotel. He went warily to his mustang, saddled and bridled it, fastened the bed roll behind the saddle, as usual. A Mexican or a half-breed was in charge. He had a sick-looking face, without expression in it except a sort of disgust. He merely said to Trainor:

"No bill for you to pay, eh, señor? Eh, and that's the luck!"

Even the stableman knew that he was picked out for slaughter. But it was apparent that if he chose to ride away from Alkali at this moment, there would be no more trouble. If he stayed there, he was to be dead before morning.

So, as he turned the horse out onto the street, where it broke into a little shamble, trotting meagerly with the forefeet and walking with the hind, he tried to think this thing out to a conclusion. They would start looking for him, before long. As soon as Cormack or Josh May delivered a report, they would begin the search, and then he would be only a few moments from death.

Where would they search for him?

That question drove him straight toward a desperate resolution. They might comb the entire town, but they were not likely to think of searching in the Golden Hope, any more than bees would search for danger in their own hive.

A cold hand gripped his heart when he thought of the peril of entering the place. But, after all, he had to see Doc Yates. He had to try to wring information out of that master mind. And though he told himself that the thing was impossible, and that he was giving himself from the frying pan into the fire, back towards the Golden Hope he turned his horse.

He did not go directly. He found an empty field, and in the field a cluster of little second-growth trees in the center of which he tied his mustang. From that point he turned up the back street, through the alley, and arrived at the rear door of the Golden Hope.

There was not a single light across the broad shoulders of the place, but plenty of light came from the inside. He could distinguish the laughter in the barroom. He could hear the music and the foot shuffling out of the dance hall adjoining, which must by this time be going full blast. To run such a place, Doc Yates must have a score of retainers, in one capacity or another. To break in on that man would be like—

He took hold of the knob of the rear door and pushed it, knowing that it must be locked. Instead, it opened and admitted him readily. He found himself in a narrow hallway, lighted by a smoking lamp that hung from the ceiling and showed the way up a dim twist of stairs.

He followed that twist, he hardly knew why, except that it took him somewhat away from the noise of the crowd. Upstairs, in the hall of the second floor, he was half-way along the ragged matting before he heard voices of men mounting behind him. One fellow laughed, and the laughter went through Trainor. What refuge? Well, there was the first door at hand. He turned the knob of it and stepped through into thick darkness.

He had a queer feeling that there had been light in the room as he started to push the door open, and that it had been extinguished suddenly, but no doubt this sprang from his having come out of the light, however obscure, in the hallway.

In the meantime, he heard the men walking down the hall outside. Sometimes their shoulders struck against the wall on either side and brought out booming, drum-like sounds. He heard their voices go by, diminishing. In another instant he could get out of this hole of darkness.

And that was when a gesture out of the darkness freed a burst of light that showed him a bedroom, a litter of women's clothes on a chair, and in the corner, in front of a dressing table with a little mirror and a lamp on it, stood a dark-haired, dark-eyed girl in a rose-colored dress. In one hand she held the cloth which she had just snatched from over the lamp. In the other hand was a revolver with its round, empty mouth pointed steadily at Trainor.

"Hello, handsome," said the girl. "What dragged you in here?"

She was one of the furnishings of the dance hall, no doubt. She had under-shadowed her eyes with a penciling too heavy, and she had made up her lips with wide, heavy strokes of red that blurred and overran at the corners, so that it looked as though she had been drinking wine carelessly, never wiping her mouth. The same carelessness was in her eyes. She could sneer or smile with equal ease, and she was sneering now.

"I got into the wrong room," said Trainor.

"Lemme put you right, brother, will you?" said the girl. "Hoist your hands and turn your face to the wall, you thief, and I'll start in putting you right! You're the dirty sneak that gets into the rooms of us girls, are you, and swipes everything you can lay your hands on? Hoist those hands, or I'll split your wishbone right in two."

He looked at her curiously. It was strange that he was not afraid, but he had come to this place with the expectation of a danger so much more vast in his mind's eye, that the sight of a girl could not move him a great deal, no matter how much bright savagery appeared in her eyes, no matter how masterfully she held the gun.

"You hear me?" she said. "You poor dummy, don't you think that I mean what I say?"

She came a couple of quick little gliding steps toward him, soft steps that would not disturb her aim at any moment.

"I hear you," said Trainor, almost drowsily. "I suppose you mean what you say."

"Then get your hands up," she commanded.

He shook his head. "I can't do that," he declared.

And then she squinted at him as she added: "What sort of an hombre are you, anyway? What are you doing in here?"

He could not think of anything except the truth. "There were some men behind me. I had to duck out of the way. This door was the closest, so I came in."

"Hi!" exclaimed the girl in a whisper. "You're one of the rummies that have been trimmed in the gambling rooms. Or they rolled you at the bar and cleaned you out. Is that it?"

"No," said Trainor. He smiled, when he thought of the immensity of difference in gravity between his motive and a mere loss of money.

"Come on, come on," she commanded patiently. "Wake up and talk, will you?"

"Well, I came here to see Yates," he said. He cursed the tongue that had spoken. But—well, after all, it made no difference. The girl would screech; in a moment armed men would come running. And then—why, he was so close to the finish that nothing mattered very much.

"Yates? You came sneaking here to see Doc?" she asked. "Wait a minute. You came here to see Doc, right in his own joint?"

"You see," said Trainor, with the same frankness, "Alkali Valley is the place of vanishing men. My brother was one of the fellows who disappeared. Maybe Doc Yates knows something about it."

"What do you know about that?" said the girl. "Right in here, where the lions are fed, too! Brother, have you ever been in this dump before?"

"I came into the saloon today," said Trainor. "That's all."

"See anything?"

"A man with my brother's pocket knife. I asked about it. We had a mix-up. He knocked me silly and threw me into the street."

"That's the red lump on the jaw, eh?" asked the girl.

"That's the one."

"You tell it straight, too," said the girl. "I heard the yarn this evening. You don't put any frills on it. Listen. Are you straight?"

"I don't know. I'm average, I hope."

"D'you know that I nearly pulled the trigger a minute ago?"

"I saw your knuckles get whiter," he agreed.

"Why didn't you shove up your hands, then?"

"I thought," said Trainor, "that I was close to the finish, anyway. As soon as you yelped, the men would come on the run, and then—" He made a wide gesture toward the window. "I wouldn't have time to get through," he said, and smiled a little.

A hand knocked on the door, a moment later.

The girl gasped, glanced from the door to Trainor, and then pointed to a quantity of dresses that hung partially revealed behind a curtain that hung from the ceiling. It was the best the room had to offer by way of a closet.

It was folly, Trainor thought, to accept the invitation, but it was better to do that than to stand there and let the unknown walk in on him. He slipped in among crinkling, whispering silks. A wave of sweet lavender filled his nostrils.

"Well?" called the girl, as the knock was repeated.

The door was pushed half open.

"I'm coming in," said a man's voice.

"Sure, Doc," said she. "Come on in, will you?"

CHAPTER VII

Black Ore

EVEN without the nickname, Trainor would have known the pale, handsome face, the youth of it, the shoulders, the black coat, the wide black hat of the man who came into the room. The bed creaked as he sat down, and Trainor, from behind the dresses, could see everything. He could jump out at the fellow, now, but if he did that, he would be betraying the girl. He had a very grim certainty, moreover, that he would never be able to surprise this man sufficiently to beat him. It would be like trying to surprise a wild beast that never sleeps with both eyes shut.

Yates was smoking a cigar. The fine, thick flavor of it came at once to Trainor's nostrils.

"I've got some news for you, Dolly," he said.

"You've always got news, and it's never good," said the

girl. She went over to her dressing glass and began to do her cheeks with dry rouge and a rabbit's foot. "What's the story this time?"

"You're hitting the hooch too hard," said Yates. "You ought to lay off that stuff."

"To please you?" she snarled.

"I don't care what you do," he answered, "only I'm telling you something that may be worth while. To you."

"Thanks," said she. "Pass the sandwiches to the hungry, Doc."

"You're a mean little devil, aren't you, Dolly?" commented Yates without emotion.

"Easy money and an easy boss to work for, why should I be mean?" asked Dolly. "That's the question."

"I've got a job for you," said Yates.

"I've got a job for you, first," answered Dolly.

"What's that?"

"It's a hard job. A bit of memory work. Tell me how many gals have broken their hearts on account of that handsome mug of yours, Doc?"

"I'm never a success with the ladies," said Yates. "Look at you. You never had any use for me."

"It's a queer thing," said Dolly. "You're the only one that I ever saw through. I don't understand it. Wait till I close that door into the hall. There's a draft through here."

"No, a couple of the boys are out there waiting," said Yates. "They'd better keep an eye on me, if you don't mind."

"You're fragile, eh?" asked Dolly. "Doc, I sure should think that you'd get tired of being trailed around by a pack of bloodhounds, licking your heels and ready to lick the other fellow's blood."

"I get my share of trouble outside of everything they can do for me," said Doc Yates. "It's years since I've had no bandages on a fresh wound. But it all pays, Dolly.

Outside of the coin, it gives me a chance to talk to the bright little girls like you."

"How I hate your rotten heart," said Dolly gently.

"Do you, darling?" asked he. "But I never hate you. I never hate a useful thing. Now I'll tell you what I want you to do. You see these?"

He held out three little white pills in the palm of his hand.

"Three sleeps for baby?" asked the girl, staring.

"That's enough to put three men to sleep, all right," said Yates. "But you use all three on one."

"You're a bright boy, Doc, but here you're up the wrong alley. I take lots of chances, but never on Salt Creek."

"Of course you don't," he agreed. "He'll get well, after he puts this stuff down his throat, but he'll sleep twenty-four hours, is all I have to say. And I want him to sleep."

"What for?" asked the girl.

"You don't mean that. You mean, what does he look like and where do you find him."

She stared grimly at Yates.

"All right," she said, "but what a hot hell you're going to burn in, Doc!"

"He's down in the dance hall, right now," said Yates. "He's drinking nothing but whisky straight, and his—"

"Then let one of your bartenders dope him."

"It can't be done. He's drinking the whisky from his own bottle, and paying full-size for the clean glasses. You're going to drop one of these into each of his next three drinks. Understand?"

"Who's he with?"

"Nobody. He's watching the dancing. The girls don't mean anything to him, but you'll mean something to him, all right."

"Maybe," admitted Dolly, not without pride. "You

want this hombre bad, Doc? But I'm not in it if there's a whang on the head for him afterward."

"We're not going to bump him off, I tell you. Go down there and spot him. Blondy, the people call him. He's as big as a house. Red hair on his wrists and yellow hair on his head. Five years too young to be in Alkali. Go down there and put him bye-bye, Dolly."

"You're not going to roll him, word of honor?"

"You little fool," said Yates angrily, "it's just a question of him knowing too much for his own good. He knows more than will ride well on his stomach. Can you make any sense out of that? He's seen something that has to do with a new strike and black ore with gold beads in it. Does that tell you enough, Dolly?"

"All right," said the girl.

A footfall ran up the hallway.

"Hey, Doc!" called a guarded voice. "He's here." A red, excited face appeared at the open door into the hall.

"Who's here?" asked Yates.

"He's here!"

"You don't mean—Wait a minute. Bring him up here. This is as good as any place. It's more unexpected. Bring him right up here! Dolly, go do your job!"

"All right," said Dolly, "but I'd like to see you with your big boss on hand. I'd like to see you taking orders."

"You know too much, and what you don't know, you guess too much about," stated Yates. "Now get out and do what you're told."

Dolly got out. From the doorway she threw one glance, half-curious and half-sneering, toward the flimsy "closet" that sheltered Trainor. And then she was gone.

Trainor's whole mind and body tightened for the effort. This might be his one moment for leaping out at Yates. But when he was leaning for the spring, he saw another man come into the hall doorway.

He thought, at first glance, that the fellow must be a

brother of Doc Yates, but then he saw the difference. This man was bigger. He had shoulders that reminded the hidden watcher of Jim Silver. His face was pale like that of Yates, but there was a difference. Ten days in the sun would put the bronze on Yates, but about this other fellow, Trainor felt that all the sun in the world would never be able to change the clear pallor of the skin. It was a very handsome face, perhaps a little too long, but the features were perfectly formed, sensitive as those of a fine artist, and above all there was a towering, massive, noble forehead. It was a face which one could not ordinarily have connected with evil, but seeing the man with Doc Yates, Trainor suddenly knew that all of the evil in the world might spring from that powerful but tainted intellect.

Yates hurried to meet the other and gripped his hand. He said:

"This is a surprise, Barry. I didn't think you'd come into town. Come in and sit down. Sorry to bring you up here into a girl's room, but I thought it might be just as well. No one would look for you here—if anybody should happen to be looking for Barry Christian, just now!"

Christian, lifting his head, looked suddenly, sternly around him, and Trainor winced back farther into his shelter. He thought nothing of the revolver in his hand. He felt totally helpless as he stared out at that man who, as the world very well knew, had been the great enemy of Jim Silver these many years. He had a strange feeling that mere bullets could not harm this devil.

"Use that name only when you have to, Yates," said Christian. Then he added, stopping short the apology which Yates started: "You've already let too many people know that I'm in this part of the world. I told you not to do that!"

"I'm sorry," began Yates, "but the fact is—"

"Never mind the facts as you see them. I'll tell you

another fact. It has to do with you and it has to do with me. Jim Silver is in the Alkali Desert!"

"Silver?" repeated Yates stupidly. "Jim Silver—down here?"

He looked half-witted, as he spoke. His mouth opened. He stooped forward a little, exactly like a man who has received a heavy blow that has half-benumbed him.

"Silver is down here, somewhere in the desert. My men have seen his wolf. That means that *I* shall see Silver, before long."

"Well, then we'll smash him, when he comes! How many are with him?"

"He seems to be alone. But he's enough, by himself. Pull yourself together, and try to start your brain working. I say that Jim Silver is somewhere near this town!"

"I follow that," said Yates. "It's a hard punch, but I can take it."

"It means we have to hurry up. You've wasted time on that fellow, and now he has to talk. You've worked with your thumbs, and not with your wits," answered Christian coldly. "There's another way to tackle the thing."

"How?" asked Yates.

"Through his sympathy," said Christian. "Any one of these noble fools can be unnerved, if you know the right nerve to press on."

"What nerve?" asked Yates.

"Use your imagination," said Christian. "There's the girl, isn't there?"

The breath left Yates in a long, soft gasp.

"Yeah! I never thought of that!" he said.

"It's time to think of it now," said Christian. "We've got to get out there now. Are you ready?"

"Of course, I'm ready."

He started toward the door, and Christian followed with a swift but leisurely step. There was such a grace about the motions of the man that Trainor found himself faintly wondering, faintly admiring. Then he saw the door close behind them, and he stepped out from his hiding place into the open room.

He had learned a vast lot; that mention of the black ore, beaded with gold, attached what he had heard to the mystery of his brother. He had a desperate suspicion that the man who must be made to talk was Clive Trainor. But he was still as far as ever from knowing where to turn himself in his quest. There was only a single dim clue, and that was "Blondy," who was to be put to sleep by Dolly in the dance hall downstairs.

CHAPTER VIII

The Clue

TRAINOR remained for a moment with his fingers fidgeting on the butt of the gun he had taken from Cormack, uncertain whether he should climb out through the window or else try to steal down through the hall and stairs, as he had come. Those nervous fingers of his made the metal rim on the center of the gun butt slide a little. He looked down immediately, half-expecting the timeworn old weapon to come apart in his hands, but now he saw that one part of the outer metal, right at the heel of the Colt, was no more than a sort of sliding clasp that played easily back and forth as soon as it was directly pressed by the finger. It revealed a hollow half the size of a walnut, and in that hollow was a closely wadded bit of paper. This he drew out, pulled it straight, and found a child's picture of a man with a round head, a stick for a body, and other sticks for arms and legs. The features were very much awry, and the tongue seemed to be sticking out. There was one word scrawled across the forehead: "Baldy!"

Trainor felt a queer touch of interest that was almost remorse. It might be that Cormack was a married man with children. All of the scoundrels are not bachelors, after all! This might have been a farewell gift from Cormack's son or daughter, and the rascal had stuffed it away in the hollow handle of his revolver. It might even be that he attached an extra importance to the scrawl, and that that was why he had been so anxious to get back his gun.

Trainor dropped the paper into his pocket and tried the window. It was well fastened, but he got it open and climbed out on the slanting roof of a shed that presently let him down to the ground just beside the dance hall. The music poured out of the shuttered windows like light; the continued whispering of the feet spoke messages to him, and every word was a warning to him to be gone. Instead, he got to a window in the rear which was open to let in a necessary draft at the expense of some privacy, and through that window he saw the picture.

There were seven or eight score of men and twenty girls. Some of the men lounged at the bar; some of them danced together, whirling rapidly; others were obviously waiting, each man, for a turn with the girls. But here and there, some girl sat out with a favored suitor, and Dolly was one, with a vast mountain of a blond man opposite her. With one hand he held her wrist. With the other hand he gripped the neck of a capacious flask. His face was bleared with a sleepy smile. He looked like a vast engine, burdened down by his own excess of weight; the sleepiness of that smile made Trainor feel that he had perhaps delayed too long already.

And suddenly he had stepped through the window. That was easy enough because it was close to the floor. The music was blaring, the dancers were a moving screen that helped to hide him from dangerous observation as he crossed to the table of Dolly. As he leaned above it, he saw her shoving a glass of whisky toward Blondy; she jerked up her head and glared at Trainor.

He knew what was in the whisky. He brushed it back from the grasp of Blondy.

"Hey!" said Blondy. "What's the main idea! Who's stealing my drinks? Who the hell is this, Dolly?"

"You big, flat-faced ham," said Dolly through her teeth to Trainor. "Back up, or I'll call a bouncer. I'll have to call a bouncer, you fool!"

Trainor gripped the shoulder of Blondy. His fingers dug through the loose outer flesh and down to a solid core of powerful muscles.

"You're being doped. Get out of here, Blondy!" he commanded.

"Hey, whatcha mean by that?" demanded Blondy.

"You're seeing double already," said Trainor. "Spread your hand and look at the fingers, and see for yourself! They're doping you."

"I'm going to squeal on you, you thick-wit!" gasped the girl. "I gotta squeal on you, if you don't get out. Look! Blackjack Harry is coming this way now. Will you run and save your hide?"

"Dope?" said Blondy stupidly, staring down at his spread fingers. "You're crazy, stranger!"

"You've seen too much—remember what you've seen!" said Trainor. "And this is the place where they're going to put you to sleep so you can't talk. Blondy, you're going to sleep on your feet!"

The screech of the girl stabbed twice through the brain of Trainor.

"You have to have it! You asked for it—take it then!" she snarled at him. "Harry! Harry! Throw this bum out!"

But Blondy had heaved himself to his feet and stood with his great legs spread.

"What I seen? Doping me? I thought that whisky had a funny taste all at once. You black-eyed vixen," said Blondy to the girl, "what you been doing?"

He reached for her, but Trainor knocked down the red fist, pulled the heavy arm over his shoulders.

Half of the dancers kept spinning on the floor. The other half had fallen into a confusion through which "Blackjack Harry" came on the run. He was that same bartender with the twisted face. He had picked up his apron as a girl might pick up her skirt to get through deep waters, and he was clawing back at his hip as he ran.

Trainor, with his free hand, scooped a chair from beside the table and flung it, underhand. Blackjack tried to duck, but he merely thrust his head into the path of the flying missile and went down, sprawling.

Then everyone started shouting. There was such a confusion of noises that Trainor felt a swirling dizziness before his eyes as he half led and half lugged the weight of Blondy toward the nearest door.

The girl grappled with Trainor. She was gasping:

"Hit me, kid! Slam me! I gotta be knocked out. I can't be suspected!"

He struck wide, with the flat of his hand, and she crumpled on the floor right in the path of the charging bouncer. The man leaped her body. Trainor backhanded him, lodging the muzzle of his gun between the eyes. He saw, from the tail of his eye, how the fellow walked backward on his heels, falling for ten feet before he struck the floor.

Then he and Blondy turned out into the side alley that ran down past the dance hall.

The fresher air seemed to give Blondy more strength. He was able to break into a run, supporting most of his own weight. They turned the corner of the building with a hue and cry behind them. They could not escape, possibly, by means of fast running, and the best Trainor could think of was to jerk Blondy back against the wall of the house.

There he stood with his wabbling burden, while five men sprinted right past them into the dark.

It was a childish device, but it had worked. He took Blondy back down the alley, turned into the rear street, and got his man out there in the tree clump, where he had left his mustang. In the central clearing, Blondy went to pieces and spilled out of the arching grip of Trainor onto the ground.

Trainor got a canteen from his saddle and threw water into the big, hot, panting face of Blondy. Still there was no response. He heaved the bulk up by the loose of the shoulders and planted him against a tree trunk. With the flat of his hand he spatted the cheeks of Blondy until his palm was burning.

Dull, confused oaths were spluttering out of the man's lips. He was going to have the heart's blood of a hound, he said. Trainor took him by the hair of the head and shook the head back and forth, knocking it heavily against the tree.

"It's life or death!" said Trainor. "It's your life, too. Try to think, Blondy. They've doped you. Try to say three words. You saw something. You saw something, and they know it. They'll murder you for it unless you tell me in time. I'm your friend, Blondy. I'm fighting for you. You saw something."

"That's why I gotta get drunk," groaned Blondy. "I seen his face. It still keeps runnin' at me, with the blood on it."

"It's not running at you. I've turned it away," pleaded Trainor. "Tell me where you saw it! Where, Blondy, where did you see it?"

"Over Baldy!" groaned the other. "Over Mount Baldy."

He groaned, and his body fell to the side.

Trainor lighted a match and looked into the swollen face. He lifted an eyelid. The eye was dull and dead-looking. He pushed Blondy on his back, opened his shirt, and listened to his heart. It beat along steadily enough, though very slowly. Probably the best thing in the world for Blondy was to be allowed to sleep out his jag, and the influence of the drug right here in the open air.

There had been only one useful word in what had been spoken—Baldy!

For that word matched the scrawl on the childish sketch which had been found in the handle of Cormack's revolver. Baldy could be a mountain, no doubt.

Trainor scratched another match and by its light re-examined the paper in his pocket. The whole thing looked different, now that he regarded it with a clue. The long lines of legs and body and arms might be trails. The queerly marked features might be natural landmarks near Baldy or on it, and the chinless, pointed dome of the head was the mountain itself. That scrawled and wriggling line was a trail, perhaps, that worked through the breast of the mountain. That right arm was the trail's continuation—for, after all, even the arm a child draws does not come out of the head of its subject. No, it might rather be a trail that went on to a forking where three trails branched out. The uppermost finger was the more extended. Yes, and at the end of it there was an arrow point, indicating that this was the right direction.

When Trainor had seen the arrow mark, he folded the paper with tender care and put it away.

He thought back over the clues as he had gathered them.

Because he had recognized his brother's knife in the hand of a stranger, he had been thrown out of the Golden Hope. He had drawn down on his head the mighty danger that flowed from Doc Yates. He had been turned out of his hotel and broadly invited to leave town through the same agency. Moreover, he had heard that something Blondy had seen had to do with a mine whose ore was like the sample he had left at the assayer's office. And Blondy had seen a frightful apparition, a man with blood on his face. Blondy was not a nervous type. He seemed to have no more sensitiveness than a great boar. And yet he had rushed for town and tried to drink himself into a stupor in order to crush the vision out of his memory.

That bleeding face began to wear, to the excited imagination of Trainor, the features of his vanished brother. He felt that his cause was lost before he embarked on the journey, because he knew that he could not hold up against such a pair as Yates and Christian, to say nothing of all their assistants.

But now he gave a farewell pat to the shoulder of the sleeper, mounted his mustang, and rode straight out of Alkali toward the hills.

CHAPTER IX

Mount Baldy

THERE were a few shacks on the edge of the town where miners lived when they were out of work or when they were tired of sledge-hammers and drills. Trainor went to the first of these in which he saw a light, and he found a pair of grizzled old veterans in their red flannel shirt sleeves, playing seven-up on top of a cracker box, bending their stiff backs painfully to take up the cards.

He dipped down from the saddle without dismounting, and looked in through the doorway.

"Partners," he said, "will you tell me the way to Mount Baldy?"

"Damn Mount Baldy," said the bald-headed one of the pair.

"Here, here, Jake," said the man with the broad beard. "That ain't no way to talk. Tell him where Baldy is, will you?"

"Shut yer mouth, Pike," said Jake. "Play the cards and shut yer mouth."

"Damning Baldy ain't no answer to him," said Pike. "It ain't a nacheral answer and it ain't a right answer."

"Why ain't it a right answer?" demanded Jake. "Ain't Baldy a hell of a place? Ain't it right to damn it?"

"Not to a stranger that's askin' his way," declared Pike.

"Perhaps you'll tell me," said Trainor to Pike, dismounting and impatiently slapping his leg with his quirt. "I'm in a hurry."

"I'd tell you free and willing," said Pike, "but there's a bigger point in this here than you think. Here, have a drink, kid."

"No, thanks," said Trainor, his very brain burning with desire to be gone. For now danger might be gathering on his trail behind him, and forming to cut him off in the distance. "I only want to know the way to Mount Baldy," he insisted.

"It's about the first time," said Pike gravely, to Jake, "that I ever seen a man refuse a drink of good corn whisky. Did you know that this was corn, young feller?"

"I'll bet it's great whisky, but I can't stop for it. I've got to get on, please!" groaned Trainor.

"I'd tell you the way in a minute," said Pike, "but there's a big idea wrapped up in this here. The idea is this: Is Jake goin' to act like a Westerner oughta act, or ain't he goin' to act that way? Is he goin' to have real hospitality, or ain't he goin' to have it? I've knowed him for a long time, and now I'd like to know this here about him."

"Shut yer old fool mouth or tell me what you bid?" demanded Jake.

"Are you or ain't you goin' to tell this here man, in a rush the way he is, the right trail to Mount Baldy?"

"Why don't the fool go and look at the mountain and ride to it?" asked Jake. "What's your bid?"

"Jake," declared Pike, putting down his cards, "this here game has gotta stop till I find out what you're goin' to do by way of showin' yourself a gentleman, or ain't you one?"

"Well, what do you wanta know?" Jake asked Trainor.

"The way to Mount Baldy," said Trainor.

"Aw, follow your nose," said Jake. "You go right on down the street and take the straight trail and don't do no branchin'. You can see Mount Baldy shinin' in the moon right now, if you got an eye in your head. Pike, what you bid?"

Trainor pitched into the saddle, and heard Pike bid two.

"I shoot the moon!" shouted Jake.

The rush of his frightened mustang carried Trainor out of earshot of the rest of the game of seven-up, and he slipped rapidly out of Alkali into the desert. There before him was a squat mountain, to be sure, with glints on it from the rising moon, as though it were formed of ice. He could imagine that there must be great, transparent cliffs of quartz. The shape of the mountain was almost a dome, though just at the top it sharpened into a pyramid.

Toward that goal he kept at a steady jog, sometimes freshening the mustang into a lope, sometimes letting it drop to a dragging dog-trot, but it was never allowed to fall to a walk until it was on the steep ascent of Mount Baldy.

The lower slopes were hills of shifting sand. He got off and trudged on foot to lighten the horse through that difficult going. Nothing lived here. Out on the desert the lifelike forms of the Spanish bayonet had been jogging past him, and great cacti like vast spiders with legs gathered, ready to spring. But even these shapes had been better than the nakedness of Mount Baldy, white under the ascending moon.

Trainor was well up on the breast of the slope before the sand ended, and he climbed into the saddle to ride on over a rocky trail. It held on, fairly straight, and then began to twist to the right.

But that was not the direction required. It was just the opposite of the trail which was marked on Cormack's sketch. Therefore, he turned back, and urged the mustang onto a higher shoulder. From the edge of a hundred-foot precipice, he glanced down, then to the sides. Finally, he spotted what he wanted, a trail that corkscrewed up the side of the mountain at just the angle which the map indicated. The moment he saw that, his heart leaped, because he became assured that the childish scratching on the paper was a map in actual fact.

He got to the beginning of that twisting trail. He followed it over the shoulder of Baldy onto a high plateau, and beside him rose a quartz cliff for hundreds of feet, brilliant, dazzling, with the quicksilver of the moonlight.

The trail went out like a light. He rode on for a quarter of a mile and still could not find it. In this blighted land there was no grass, no brush. There was nothing but the scalded face of a dead world, and the moonlight could not heal or cover its wounds.

He cut for sign, opening up in wider and wider circles. And suddenly he found the beginning of the trail again, a thin shadow that wound among the rocks.

He went on until he came to a point where the trail deepened, and again he reached a place where it spread into three forks. This was exactly the way it had been marked down on the map, so he took the farthest right-hand trail and rode along it, jogging the mustang, working his eyes rapidly here and there across the landscape to make out the least stir of life.

Yet, for all his precautions, he rode straight into the trap. He passed down a sort of gorge among enormous boulders, and as he came out on the farther side, a voice said briskly:

"Stick 'em up, brother! Grab the edge of that moon, and chin yourself on it!"

The quiet of the voice was even more convincing than the words it spoke. He heaved up his hands instantly, and the mustang stopped without a command.

Three men surrounded him. They looked very much alike—they were all big, all wore great sloppy slouch hats, all carried rifles and revolvers hanging down their thighs. Their work in life was not with picks and shovels, surely.

"Get off, and keep your hands up while you climb down," said one.

He was the fellow with the matter-of-fact voice.

Trainor obeyed, swinging one leg over the cantle and then dropping lightly to the ground.

"Your name's Trainor, eh?" asked the leader.

"Trainor?" said Trainor. "I don't know any Trainor."

"Oh, don't you? Come here, Les. Take a look at this hombre."

One of the men stepped close and pulled over the sombrero of Trainor. It was the third of that trio which had tried to murder him in the saloon, he who had come in with May and Cormack.

Trainor braced himself for the recognition.

"Why, sure it's Trainor," said Les.

"All right," said Trainor, "you can call me any name you like. Bud is what I answer to, mostly. If you boys are looking for hard cash, take my wallet. There's something in it; not much. But let me get my arms down before they break off at the shoulders."

"Maybe something more than your shoulders is due to be broke," said the leader. "Get his gun, Les."

The gun of Cormack was instantly taken. Would they recognize him through that, also?

But for the present no one paid any attention to it, except that Les said:

"This hombre fans it. I didn't think that he was that good."

"If you're not Trainor," said the leader, "what's your real name?"

"Bud is what I answer to, mostly, but a couple of times in my life I've been called Mr. Somerville."

The leader chuckled a little. "That ain't so bad," he said. "You sound all right to me, kid, but this is a busy night. Listen to me, Les," he added. "By what we know about Trainor, he's an ordinary cowhand. He wouldn't 'a' had the time to waste learning how to fan a gun, would he?"

"No. That sort of stops me."

"Sure of his mug?"

"I wouldn't be sure of that," admitted Les. "When I had my eye on Trainor, he was moving pretty fast, and there was a flock of guns in the air. You know how it is. You just get a kind of quick impression, at a time like that."

"If you're not Trainor, what you doing up here on this trail, Bud?" asked the leader.

"I'm on the way to Mount Baldy," said Trainor calmly.

"Yeah, and then where? Going to camp at the spring?"

"I didn't know there was any spring," said Trainor. "Fact is, I'm bound for Alkali to try to get a job. They say some of the old mines are opening up big."

The leader was silent for a moment.

"This sounds all right," said Les.

"Yeah, it sounds all right," said the leader. "You're on the wrong trail, Bud," he added, almost kindly. "If you turn around and shove straight back, you'll come to Baldy, and you'll get a trail down him for Alkali. Here, Les, give him back his gun. He's all right."

In fact, the leader reached for the gun to pass it back. But as he grasped it, he started violently.

"By thunder!" he shouted. "That's Cormack's gun!"

That was the end, Trainor knew. But he had gone into action the instant he saw the start of the leader. He made one step forward and slung himself along the side of his mustang, which bolted straight up the slope. One foot had found the stirrup. The other leg was hooked around behind the cantle, one arm was curved over the neck of the pony. He could thank his stars that he had learned that Indian trick when he was a youngster, for now he offered to his enemy only the mark of a running horse.

CHAPTER X

The Search

THEY had rifles after him in a moment. The spattering of the revolver shots had given him an instant of hope, for the way the mustang was dodging among big rocks, he had a reasonable guess that they might keep on missing their target. But when they opened up with rifles, he knew the trouble was on him.

He heard, he almost felt, the sickening spat of the bullets as three of them in rapid succession hit the poor little horse. It went on, staggering, wavering, but still at a gallop. It reached the top of the slope before the crash of three guns at once dropped it like a stone, dead.

Trainor rolled headlong down the steep of the slope, found a nest of rocks, ran straight through it as fast as he could bolt, and then, with the rattling of the hoofs of approaching horses beating in his ears, he threw himself right down in the open. There was merely a shallow scoop in the flat of the rock, and he flung himself down in full view of anyone whose curious eyes might examine differences inside that meager shadow. In fact, the full moonshine was beating down upon most of his body, but the chance he took was that the enemy might not search for him at all in such an open spot.

Over the ridge he saw them come hurtling, right beside the spot where his horse lay dead. They scanned the ground there, as though hoping that they might find him pinned to the ground. Then they scattered out and rode around in a circle, the leader taking one side of the big arc, Les and the other man taking the second half of the circumference. They covered a margin much larger than a man could possibly have reached on foot in the short time that had been at the disposal of Trainor. He admired, grimly and grudgingly, the manner in which the search was conducted, as he saw the riders skilfully wind back and forth and in and out among the rocks. He could thank his instinct that he had not chosen to secrete himself among those obvious shelters.

The leader, rising in his stirrups presently, shouted to the men to go back on the ground and try again. The man had to be there. He must be there.

So they went back, again, and yet again, and widened the field of their search, and then assembled in a close group, the hoofs of their horses lifting and gleaming not five paces from the spot where Trainor lay flat on his face, waiting every dreadful moment for bullets to tear through his flesh.

The leader said: "Les, you might have used your eyes back there in the saloon."

"I thought it was him when I first looked, but he was so damn cool," said Les. "You know how it is. I saw him by lamplight, movin' fast, and this was by moonlight, standin' still. And then he didn't give away no chances. He's a nervy hombre."

"I'll nerve him if I can daub a rope onto him," said the leader. "Where'd he go to, anyway?".

"Suppose," said the third man, "that he was layin' there close to the hoss, somewheres right by the ridge? We might 'a' galloped over that ridge a mite too fast, and he sneaked off down the other side?"

"He couldn't 'a' done it," answered the leader.

"Well, where else is he?"

"It's the damnedest thing that I ever seen. Let's go back to the ridge and take a look-see."

They climbed up the slope to the ridge and sat there against the moon, black, gigantic silhouettes. Their voices came small but clear to the ears of Trainor.

"Where could he 'a' gone? Why, back there through the rocks, down the slope. That's the only thing that he could 'a' done. It's dead certain that we'd 'a' found him if he's been over yonder. He's scuttlin' off a coupla miles away, by this time. No matter what else we did, we scared the shirt right off his back, and I'm dead sure of that!"

"Don't be too sure of nothin'. This hombre seems soft, don't he? Sure he seems soft when he walks into the picture. Blacky says that there wasn't nothin' to him. Blacky says that he pretty nigh busted the neck of Trainor, and throws him into the street, and Trainor goes and hollers to the sheriff. That sounds soft, don't it? Well, maybe Trainor was soft when he come to Alkali, but he ain't soft now. He's walked right through Yates, it looks like, and got out here. He's slammed May and Cormack in one little go, and they're tough hombres. Besides all that, how in hell did he learn that this was the trail to foller?"

There was no answer, and the leader said: "Maybe he ain't scuttlin' off through the rocks, doin' a mile a minute. Maybe he's sneakin' up toward headquarters. And if he gets there—boys, Christian is goin' to take off our hides in chunks and burn them right in front of our eyes!"

"What'll we do, then?"

"Go straight back, search all along the way, and make a report that we met Trainor, and that we lost him, but we hope that he's scared off."

There was a silence, then one of the others said: "You can do that job, Perry. I don't hanker to stand up to Christian when he's sour. I seen him sour just once, and that was enough for me."

They rode suddenly over the ridge. They disappeared, and the hoofbeats of the horses rang farther and farther away as Trainor rose to his feet. Luck, he saw, had at last given him a golden chance, for the beating hoofs of those horses were like so many bells, guiding him on the way he wanted to go—if only he were able to keep them within hearing.

In spite of the fact that he had spent such a share of his life in the saddle, he could run, and he ran now, keeping his chin down and his arms swinging straight. He got the sound of the hoofbeats before him, now dim, now closer, now suddenly far away.

His high-heeled boots, the worst running gear in the world, he jerked off and threw away. He ran on in his thick socks and now and again a rock point tore his flesh. He merely gritted his teeth and lengthened his stride.

If this were the worst pain that he ever had to endure, it would be very well. If he had to run till his feet were worn to the bone, he would do that, also.

He could remember in his boyhood when Clive had run for him and climbed for him—yes, and fought for him, too. He could remember how they had stood back to back and held off the savage little mob when they went to the new school in the mountains. He could remember how Clive had stood by to see fair play when he had his celebrated fight with "Stew" Murphy, and how Clive had knocked flat the bully who tried to trip Ben up in the middle of the go. He could remember days when they were older, and always it had been Clive who came to the rescue.

Now he had his chance to pay back a little portion of the old debt. Even if there had been no debt at all, there was the claim of blood that gripped him. The home was gone. Their mother and father had been dead for years, and that was all the more reason for them to hang together in this world.

Yet he felt helpless. He was running hard, he was running toward his duty. But what would he be able to accomplish when he got there? What could he do against Christian and Doc Yates? The mere thought of them made him feel like a child.

He dropped suddenly flat on the ground, for he had entered a naked valley, without rocks, and the three riders were in clear view before him. When he looked up again, they had disappeared!

He got slowly to his knees, thinking that his wits were gone, that he had been dazzled by a hallucination. Not only were the figures gone, but the hoofs no longer rang bell-like on the rocks, or muffled on hard ground. He leaped up and ran on again, bewildered. It might be that they had glimpsed him and had scattered to the shadow at the left of the valley, waiting for him to come on, but somehow, that seemed a small risk. If he missed this way, he would have lost the chance to follow the trail to the end, and he would have lost it forever, perhaps.

Then, when he came close to the spot where they had seemed to be before vanishing, he saw, suddenly, a narrow cleft in the high, sheer wall of the valley. How deep the crevice went he could not tell. But into this, surely, the three must have passed.

There was almost utter darkness within the lips of the close ravine. He had to look up toward the sky to see how the opening ran between its crooked walls. Then, turning a sharp corner, he came on quite another prospect, for the crevice opened into a fair-sized gulley, sand-bottomed. That sand had hushed the hoofs of the horses, of course. And still the thin dust which they had raised in passing hung in the air, and was acrid and tingling in his nostrils.

He climbed the easy slope. The moon brightened on it. He could see where the horses had stepped not long before, and the sand was still running down the sides of the depressions. Now, topping the slope, he saw a thin, yellow eye of light, and made out, at once, a cluster of small buildings that were apparently made of rock, flat-roofed, squat, and low. In front of the one shack which was lighted, he saw three horses, with riders in the saddles of two, and with the other of the trio standing in front of the door of the hut.

Trainor could hear the knocking of the hand as he dropped to his knees and crawled off to the side until he gained the shelter of a little mesquite which managed to send its roots down to water even through this sandy hell. In that meager shadow he lay flat, for he heard the squeaking of hinges, and then the voice of none other than Barry Christian, inquiring:

"Who's there?"

"Perry," came the answer.

"Perry, will you kindly tell me what you mean by being away from the place where I posted you?"

"Because Trainor came up that way—"

"Trainor, eh? Where did you bury him?"

"That's what I want to explain. We got him, and took his gun, and had him helpless—"

"And he got away? Perry, you mean to say that he got away?"

"I don't know how to say it, chief. The fact is that he nearly fooled us, for a minute, and just as I made out for sure that he was really Trainor, he jumped for his horse, and rode the side of it like an Indian, and we shot the horse down, and went in search of him, but he managed to melt himself right into the ground. I never saw anything like it. It might have beaten even you, chief."

There was a silence, a dreadful silence for Perry, no doubt.

Then Christian said, his voice muffled by the control he put upon his passion: "It's the first big thing I ever asked you, and you've failed, Perry. But go down now and guard the mouth of this ravine, here. You were on horses and he was on foot. I suppose he couldn't have got here before you?"

"We came as fast as the rocks would let us. He couldn't have got here before us."

"Then go down there and watch for him, and if you get your hands on him the second time, smash him like a snake. He's got to die!"

CHAPTER XI

A Familiar Voice

As the three riders went slowly down the slope of sand, Trainor said the same thing to himself. He had to die. There was no way out for him. He had taken up the fight against too many men, and men of a caliber too large for him, and he had to go down.

Now, from behind the mesquite, he saw the three riders pass, and his heart shrank when they came to that point where he had dragged himself across the sand, because under the brilliance of the moon the marks must have been perfectly clear to show his course right up to the mesquite. But those three riders seemed to be thinking forward and looking forward. They paid no attention to the ground they were riding over, but went down into the narrow shadows of the gulch beneath.

That new escape let Trainor breathe again. His nerves had not stopped shuddering when, through the open door of the stone hut, he heard the voice of a man call out, in an agony, words of protest that shambled together without syllabication. There was no need of making out the words to understand the appeal, but what lifted Trainor from behind the mesquite and started him running forward, suddenly, was that he recognized the voice of his brother.

The rush of savage emotion brought Trainor right up to the hut before good sense checked him again. He dropped to his knees beside the broken shutters of a window and looked in upon things that made his brain spin dizzily.

It was a room of very respectable size. In the very old days, perhaps as far back as the time of the Spanish occupation, this must have served as headquarters for the chief . engineer of the abandoned mine whose mouth opened black in the side of the cliff behind this house. The sandy slope up which Trainor had just come was no more, as he could see it now, than the ancient dump of the mine, which had half filled the ravine. The sand itself was a mere facing which had been put on by a more recent century.

The room held one relic of its old importance—a huge table a dozen feet in length with carved legs and a great carved spanner. It must have been hauled out here at incredible cost of labor, perhaps at the demand of a wife of that unlucky man who was named master of the mine in the middle of this desert. Since then, it had been scarred with spurs and whittled with knives, but even so, only the edges were deformed. At one end of this table now sat Barry Christian, with Yates beside him. The similarity between them struck Trainor again—the same pale and handsome features. They might be brothers. Or perhaps the highest evil had to be cast much in the same form.

Opposite them, his hands roped before him, stood a haggard ghost of a man with a blood-soiled bandage about his head and with frightfully staring eyes. His clothes were in rags; through the rents Trainor could see purple welts and raw places, half scabbed over. Off at the side of this picture was a sandy-haired girl whose blue eyes were desperately fixed before her. And Blacky held both her wrists in the grasp of one capacious hand.

"You heard me, Trainor," said Christian.

Ben Trainor started violently as he heard his name, but the parched lips of the ragged skeleton inside the hut answered:

"I heard you, Christian. But you wouldn't go through with it."

"Wouldn't I?" said Christian. He smiled, looked aside at Yates, and pulled out a cigar and lighted it. He said, through the blue-gray clouds of smoke that left his lips: "He doesn't think that I'll go through with it, Doc."

Yates turned a bit in his chair.

"Give her a crack or two with the whip, to warm her up, Blacky," he commanded.

Blacky, straightway lifted the short-lashed quirt and stiffened the arm that held the girl away from him. Then, over his shoulder, he said:

"All right, chief. But if the gal screeches, maybe Perry and the rest will come peltin' up here. They wouldn't want nothin' to happen to a gal. Some gents are funny, that way. They wouldn't want nothin' to happen."

"If they come pelting up here, they'll go pelting back again, damned pronto," answered Yates. "Do what you're told to do and stop the talking."

"It's all the same to me," said Blacky. "Male or female, what the hell do I care?"

He stood back, measuring the girl, but the sleep-walking stare in her eyes had not changed in the least. And Ben Trainor, looking at the horror in the face of his brother, had to set his teeth to keep from groaning. From a shed behind the house, he heard a sudden trampling and snorting of horses. It seemed as though even dumb brutes were protesting against this thing that was about to be.

"Give it to her!" commanded Christian, turning suddenly in his chair, half rising.

The hand of Blacky swung back with the quirt, but the cry that came out of Clive Trainor was such a wild scream that it stopped the stroke.

"I'll talk, Christian!" he yelled. "Don't touch her. I'll tell you where the mine is. I'll tell—"

He tried to run around the corner of the table, but he struck the projecting angle and even that shock was enough to throw him off his balance. He fell heavily to the floor and lay still. The girl dropped to her knees and covered her eyes with one arm.

"Shall I whang her?" asked Blacky, his brutal face looking over his shoulder for orders.

"What's the use, if that half-wit will talk, at last?" said Christian. "Doc, take a look at him and see if the fool is alive."

Yates went to the fallen body and with a thrust of his foot turned it on its back. He kneeled and put his hand over the heart of Clive Trainor. There was a long, sick moment during which Ben Trainor waited for the report.

"All right," said Yates. "Not much to it, but it's still beating, all right."

He stood up, picked a canteen from the table, and emptied a quantity of water over the prostrate man.

"That'll bring him to," said Yates. "You were right about the girl, Barry. I would have put her through her jumps, sooner or later, but I never would have thought of doing it in front of Trainor. It broke him right up. And yet there's a nervy fellow, Barry. But he crashed when he saw the girl about to get it."

"Here, you, Nell!" commanded Christian. "Stand up."

The girl did not move.

"Get her up on her feet," said Christian.

Blacky took her by the hair of the head and lifted her up. She stood wavering before them, with the same unconscious look in her eyes.

"Now that your man is ready to talk and tell us where the mine is," said Christian, "why don't you save him the trouble and tell us yourself?"

She stared before her, unanswering. Her eyes seemed

to find those of Ben Trainor beyond the broken shutters.

"She's out of her head," said Yates. "Maybe the gal loves this Clive Trainor. Maybe she's off her nut, Barry."

"Maybe, maybe," said Christian carelessly. "Lock the girl in that back room again, Blacky, and throw Trainor out into the open. The fresh air may bring him back. Lies there like a dead snake, doesn't he?"

Blacky pushed the girl through another door and locked it after her. He went to Clive Trainor and bent to get a grip on the hair of his head. That seemed to be Blacky's favorite grip. Perhaps it was in that manner that he, Ben Trainor, had been dragged out of the Golden Hope and so dropped into the dust of the street.

In the same way he dragged Clive Trainor, now, to the threshold of the hut, pausing there to say, over his shoulder:

"Two tough hombres, in their own ways. I mean, these here Trainor brothers."

"Tough, a little tough," agreed Yates, "but they're being softened, little by little. Drop him out there and fan him with something."

"I'll fan him, all right." Blacky laughed, as he disappeared through the door with his burden.

"Where could that other Trainor be?" wondered Yates.

"I don't know," answered Christian. "Perry hasn't heard the last about that case. When a man fails me once, he never has a chance to fail me again—unless it's Jim Silver that he slips on."

"Ah, well," said Yates. "Silver's different, of course." Then he added heartily: "You'll get him if he puts his head too close to our affairs, down here. Even a Jim Silver can't manage an organization like the one you've built up here, Barry."

"He's a rock that's broken some big machines," said Christian calmly. "But I've an idea, Doc, that the time may be coming when I'll have my turn of luck with him. There's one queer thing about it. If I had him in my hands, I wouldn't quite know what to do with him."

"I know some Indian ways that you'd be pretty much interested in," said Doc Yates.

Christian shook his head, answering: "He's smashed me half a dozen times. There was a day, Doc, when hundreds of hard men were ready to ride the instant that I lifted a finger. But that day has gone by. Because Silver has shown people, over and over again, that I can be broken. He's had me in jail more than once, with the rope practically around my neck. But each time I've managed to get out from under and now I think that I may be able to have my innings. How will I take them? With fire or water or steel? I don't know. If there were a hundred of him, Doc, I'd need to use up all of his bodies to carry out some of the ideas that I have."

"You can't tell," said Doc Yates. "I may be there to give you some inspiration."

There was a loud, continuous clapping sound outside the front door.

"See what that is," said Christian.

Yates went to the door and called out:

"Stop that, Blacky! I told you to fan him, not beat him to death."

He turned and came back toward Christian.

"The blighter was whanging Trainor on one side of the face and then on the other," he reported.

Ben Trainor waited to see and hear no more. Right at his feet there was a stone that had fallen out of the old wall. He picked up the weight and walked with it to the corner of the house. There he could see Blacky. That gentle soul even now was not fanning the helpless man on the ground. Instead, he had taken a good grip on the hair of his head and was twisting it slowly and powerfully.

Trainor made one long step forward, swayed the stone, and brought it down heavily on the thick skull of Blacky. He slumped noiselessly beside his victim.

CHAPTER XII

Pursuit

THE yellow arm of lamplight reached the boots of Clive, the outflung arm of Blacky. Perhaps the two men inside the hut could see that much of the scene outside. Ben Trainor drew the two Colts from Blacky's holsters. He wanted to turn to the doorway of the house and open fire. One of the pair he would surely get with his first bullets; perhaps he could be sufficient benefactor of mankind to kill them both.

But what of that?

Down there in the neck of the ravine were three more armed men, practiced fighters, who would come like wolves at the sound of the firing, and he knew that he could not play his hand against the three of them. They would murder him, and finish the nearly completed job on Clive Trainor.

So Ben Trainor handled the great temptation for only an instant. Then he put up the two revolvers and lifted the body of Clive from beside the fallen gunman. He saw a great gash across Blacky's skull, and there was enough light to show him the running blood. Vaguely, he remembered having heard that blood will not run after a man is dead. Perhaps he ought to deal one more blow before he tried to escape, but the thought of crushing the skull of the inert body sickened him.

He held the body of Clive in his arms, the head and arms and feet trailing down. It seemed to him that there was not half the weight that should have been in the bulk of a grown man. He could feel the wasted, bony frame he was bearing, as he rounded the further corner of the stone hut.

Right before him was a shed out of which came sounds of feeding horses and the sweet fragrance of hay. He laid Clive on the soft sand and went inside. He could make out the forms of six horses by favor of the moonlight that sloped in through the open door and a window. The big gray, most visible in this light, he started saddling at once, and the tall horse turned its head and sniffed at him curiously, without fear. It seemed to Ben Trainor like an omen of good fortune.

A knocking commenced inside the house. He heard it clearly, and also the voice of Christian, calling:

"Well, what is it now?"

"Will you let me take care of him?" said the voice of the girl.

If she would only be still, if she would stay in her place, perhaps Trainor could get her away with Clive. But the devil of bad luck was making her spoil her own chances.

"Take care of him? I don't know why," said Christian. "He's got Blacky out there taking care of him now, and you know what a good nurse Blacky is!"

"Hello, Blacky!" called Yates. "How are things going?"

Trainor, with desperate, trembling fingers threw the saddle on the back of the next horse.

"He won't answer," said Yates, after a moment. "The sulky brute won't speak up till he's brought his man around."

"A form of professional pride, and you ought to be glad that he has it," said Christian easily.

"If you'll let me out, if you'll let me take care of him," pleaded the girl, "I'll tell you whatever you want to know.

Let me go to him, and I'll tell you everything you wish—
things that he doesn't know!"

"There's an idea, chief," muttered the voice of Yates.

"Perhaps it is," said Christian. "Bring her out here."

Hinges creaked.

"You've come back to life and sense, have you, Nell?"
said the voice of Christian, with a sort of sneering gentle-
ness in it. "You can see, Doc, that we ought to have
played these two beauties off against one another a long
time ago. You want this fellow, Trainor, do you, Nell?"

"I want to help him," said the girl. Her voice went to
pieces: "Don't you see that he's dying?"

The voice and the words curdled the blood of Ben
Trainor as he turned and led the pair of horses toward
the wide doorway.

"Oh, he's a tough lad," said Christian. "He'll get all
right, with a good nurse. You and Clive are going to
marry at the end of the romance, eh?"

"No," said the girl. "Let me go to him now."

"Steady, steady," said Christian. "We have to have
a little bargain first. I want your solemn oath, Nell. Raise
that sweet little right hand in the air and swear that you'll
tell us everything that will help us to the mine, after
we've let you go to Trainor."

"I'll swear it. I *do* swear it!" said she.

Trainor, lifting the weight of his brother, heard the
voices dimly. He slid one of Clive's legs into the stirrup.
He laid the loose weight of the body forward on the saddle, and then thanked his fortune that these were not
wild, dancing mustangs, but big horses, well-trained, gentle as lambs even in the hands of strangers. One step forward on the part of the gray would dislodge that helpless
burden. For one instant, Ben Trainor lingered, his hand
pressed over the heart of his brother until he was assured of the feeble flickering of the pulse. Then he
mounted the bay horse he had saddled for himself and

brought it close to the gray. He managed both pairs of reins with one hand. With the free hand he raised the limp torso of Clive and supported it.

Dimly, inside the house, he could hear the girl crying out that she would make any promises they wished, if only they would let her come to Clive Trainor.

And Clive Trainor, in the meantime, was being taken slowly forward up the continuing slope of the sand, and now over the head of it and toward better footing below, where the high plateau rolled gradually down toward the desert—a vast sweep of land that looked as though the wreckage and the fragments had been cast over it when the higher mountains to the south were first created. Boulders larger than houses rose up, here and there, and now stones and clean rock gritted under the shod hoofs of the horses.

Could even Barry Christian and Yates follow the trail over such a hole-in-the-wall country as this?

Then, from over the sandy brows of the hill, Trainor heard a trio of revolver shots in quick succession. He heard shouting that seemed horribly close. And far down the ravine, he heard an answering Indian yell.

He got the horses into a trot that jounced Clive horribly in the saddle. He put them into a soft lope, at which, strangely enough, he could manage the loose burden of his brother's weight much better. And now the boulders were drifting behind them, thickening like the trunks of trees as one enters a wood, throwing up to their rear a screen which no human eye could see through.

But, in the meantime, five keen and savage men were on the way. Three of them would rush out in the van. Christian and Yates would follow as soon as their flying hands could fling saddles on the backs of their horses. Or would one of them remain behind to make sure of the girl?

The sound of her voice remained in the ear of Ben

Trainor like a sweet taste in the throat, and the blue, blank stain of her eyes, remembered now, made him want to turn back and try his chance of dodging through the enemy and coming to her help.

He made himself put that temptation out of his mind.

He went on, with the great stones moving about him, until he heard in the distance the sound of beating, galloping hoofs. At that, he was tempted to flog the horses into full speed. But he could not handle them if they went too fast. He could not dare to let them keep at a canter, or even a trot, for fear the noise they made would come to the ears of the man hunters. With all his soul straining forward, anxious to make haste, he had to bring the horses down to a walk. That was the way they went forward, side by side, the arm of Ben Trainor strained about the body of his brother, and the head of Clive wavering on the support of Ben's shoulder.

The face that the moon showed to the younger brother was a horrible thing. A new trickle of blood had commenced from beneath the head bandage, and it ran slowly down the cheek and dripped off the chin. The mouth of Clive hung open, and the loose jaws worked, and the teeth clicked, now and then, moved by the swaying of the horses, until there was a horrible semblance of munching food, continually.

It seemed to Ben Trainor that he could not endure the strain of the thing any longer. The noise of the riders, swinging this way and that around him, beat into his brain like so many lines of fire, but the danger was nothing compared with this monstrous ride with a dying man.

He saw, not far before him, the gleam of water under the side of a mighty rock that rose like a cliff from the ground. Well, speed would not save them, anyway. Only chance could rescue them from the eyes of Christian and his men, and, therefore, they might as well halt here—

and hope. After all, they had covered enough ground to prevent the men of Christian from quartering the space between that and the deserted mine and combing every bit of it, thoroughly.

Into the shadow of the rock, therefore, Ben rode, and tied the horses to a projecting knob of stone. Then he slid the entire lower part of Clive's body into the pool, and drew him out again upon the dry land.

He dropped flat, and listened to the heartbeat. It was feeble, very feeble, and there were frightful pauses into it that seemed like death itself, but always the slow thumping or the uncertain fluttering began again.

He sat up and considered the wan, starved face of his brother. Pain had fretted it deeply. Pain had worn it away.

He looked up, suddenly, at the sky where the moon had put out the stars, and he wondered what hell on earth or hereafter could be sufficient for men like Yates and Barry Christian.

Then, in a voice that seemed to come from a great distance, he heard Clive speaking. It was a low muttering. It increased to a clear sound. It grew into a shout!

"Be quiet!" pleaded Ben Trainor. "Clive, you're safe. I've got you away from them. Be still or you'll have them on us!"

For close, terribly close, he heard the beating of hoofs. But Clive Trainor, with the face of a madman, strove to struggle to his feet.

Ben clapped a hand over the mouth that gaped to screech. Straightway his brother's teeth bit his hand to the bone, and the cry, half-stifled, rose into the night.

For both their sakes, with an agony in his heart, Ben Trainor struck down the delirious man, and then held the crumpling body in his arms. With a steady beat, he heard the cantering hoofs of a horse sweep straight toward him.

CHAPTER XIII

The Rifleman

THERE were other riders in the distance, trailing noises here and there, but this horseman came on with a frightful directness. The clanking hoofs pounded nearer. They thundered in the very ears of Ben Trainor. As he pulled one of Blacky's guns, he looked up at the lofty silhouette of a rider who was swinging around the corner of the very boulder that sheltered them.

It was the tall figure of the gunman named Perry, who sat in the saddle, pulling his horse back on its haunches, and whipping out a revolver. So the two confronted one another. Trainor, to be sure, had the drop, but the noise of a gunshot would be certain to draw in the rest of the searchers. Perry stared down bewildered at the crouched body at the verge of the pool.

"By thunder," said Perry. "You got him, did you?" He pointed to the limp body of Clive. He pointed to the horses.

"You got him—and the hosses to pack him on—from Christian and Yates. You knocked Blacky cold as a cork. And here you are, by the jumping thunder!" said Perry.

Deliberately he put up his revolver.

He pulled off his hat and mopped his brow. The mustang walked on, unguided, toward the pool, entered it knee-deep, and drank. And Perry paid no heed.

"I dunno what to do, and you dunno what to do," said Perry. "If you plug me, those other hombres hear the gun, and that's that. If I try to grab you, you drop me anyway. If I ride off from here, you can't stop me without shootin' and you daren't to shoot. But if I ride off from here and turn in a gent that's gone through hell for the sake of his brother, I'll burn an extra thousand years with sulphur up my nose."

He jammed his hat on his head again.

"Perry," said Trainor, "pull off from them. Get out of the gang. Christian doesn't mean well by you. When I was at the hut, I heard him say that a man who failed him once was no good to him. He'll make you pay for it, Perry."

"Maybe he will," said Perry. "But you think I could pull out of this? You talking about me going straight?"

"It's a big world. You could go places."

"No," said Perry grimly, "I've sold out, and I gotta stay sold."

Trainor said nothing. He waited. Fear was in him, around him, and yet there was room for a quick and strange pity for this man.

"Well," said Perry at last. "I'm doggoned if I know. If things had broke different, I'd 'a' been glad to pump you full of lead and get myself famous with Christian, that way. But the way things are breaking, I dunno. What the hell? I didn't see you, and that's about all there is to it."

He pulled his horse out of the pool and turned it away.

"So long, and get whatever kind of luck is left for you, Trainor," he muttered. He put his horse to a canter and was gone, swinging rapidly away from sight among the great rocks.

Just then Clive Trainor opened his eyes, and the madness was gone out of them. He looked straight up into the face of his brother and sighed. "You know, Ben," he muttered, "I've been having a dream with a girl and a gold mine and Barry Christian and a lot of other stuff wrapped up in it."

He raised his hand to his bandaged head, and groaned slightly.

"Ben, was it all true?" he asked.

"All true, but steady, old son," said Ben Trainor.

"Where are we? What happened? I was back there in the stone house by the old mine and Blacky was going to—"

He groaned again.

"He didn't put the whip on the girl," said Ben Trainor. "You started around the edge of the table, and bumped into it—and you fell and were knocked out. That's all that happened. They threw you out on the sand with Blacky to fan you back to life. I had a chance to slam him, get you on one of the horses, and here we are. Steady, Clive. They're all around us. They might spot us at any minute. You can hear their horses. Here comes one now!"

The clangor of the hoofs bore straight down on them, grew to overwhelming volume, and then passed on, the rider unseen.

"And Nell?" said Clive, pulling at his brother.

"I couldn't get at her. They had her in talking to them. I had to come away. I'm sorry. It burns me up to think of leaving her behind, but I couldn't stay."

"She's gone then," said Clive, closing his eyes. "I sort of knew from the first time I laid eyes on her that she wouldn't pull through with it. There was something too sort of clean about her. That kind doesn't get to happiness, nor money, either. She's so white, Ben, that I never knew a white woman before her—except mother. And now she's gone."

"Maybe not," said Ben Trainor eagerly. "We're not finished, Clive. It's a game I'll hang onto as long as you will. I've got to get you into a better spot than this, and then I'll find help to come back."

"They'll be gone like birds," said Clive. "But—"

He shut his teeth with a click and said no more.

In the meantime, all the noises of iron hoofs on hard rock had ceased for the moment.

"Can you sit a saddle, with a little help?" asked Ben.

"I'll try. I'm a little done in, Ben, but I'll do what I can."

When he was lifted up onto the horse, he was able to swing a leg across the saddle and then settle his feet into the stirrups. He gathered up the reins.

"Have you got a drink with you?" he asked.

"Not a drop."

"Maybe it's better without the stuff," said Clive. "The strength a fellow gets out of a bottle burns out fast enough. I can ride, Ben, but not fast."

"Here's my arm," said Ben Trainor. "I'm right here beside you, and you can't fall. We'll walk them. That's the best we can hope for."

And that was how they dragged across the boulder-strewn plateau, walking the horses, while Clive gripped the pommel of his saddle with both hands and endured as well as he could. Sometimes weakness made him sway dangerously, but when the hand of Ben had saved him, he always found a new reservoir of strength which he could call upon for the next few moments.

Twice they halted for a brief rest, with Clive Trainor stretched flat on the ground, breathing with a little rattling groan in the back of his throat. But he made no complaints. He did not refer again to Nell and her fate. His suffering, his weakness, he kept to himself, until failing strength made him waver almost to falling.

Ben Trainor, all this time and into the pink of the dawn, was equally silent. Words were not of any use to Clive, and words would not express what Ben felt about this quiet man.

Afterwards, he might learn what had actually happened while Clive was in the hands of Christian and the others. About that, Ben was not curious. Christian and Yates needed burning alive. That much was already certain. And for the rest, Ben wanted nothing except to get his brother to safety.

There was no refuge for them on the plateau. They would have to get down onto the desert and hope to be able to cut across it to the town of Alkali, though surely that was like jumping from the frying pan into the fire. But there was no other alternative.

A doctor was surely needed for Clive. And help—if help could be found in Alkali—for the girl.

There was no certainty. There was no real safety, as yet. And the beauty of the dim sunrise over the desert was lost upon the eye of Ben Trainor as he and his brother rode down the steep pitch of a trail that brought them onto the sandy flat of the desert.

They came through the narrow jaws of the gorge that had ushered them down from the plateau, but before they were a quarter of a mile out into the open, Ben Trainor saw a stream of five riders sweeping toward him, close to the cliffs, aiming to cut him off from a retreat and shunt him out onto the desert where he and Clive would be quick and easy prey. What good was the strength of their horses when three strides at full gallop would throw Clive out of the saddle, in spite of all that Ben could do?

They had to turn. Ben shouted to rouse Clive out of his deadly torpor. Then back they fled, daring no more than a rolling, easy canter, while those five hawks were coming at them across the sands.

First came Barry Christian. It seemed to Ben Trainor that he could have selected the man from ten million, even though all were, like Yates, almost exactly similar to him. There was something joyous and light and alert in his bearing in the saddle. There was something in the keen evil of his spirit that made his horse run more swiftly than the rest.

Right back at the mouth of the canyon through which they had just come, Ben Trainor now aimed their course. Christian, riding at unabated speed, put a rifle to his shoulder and started firing to head off the fugitives.

It seemed impossible that he should be able to hit any mark, as he sat a galloping horse, but hornet sounds of danger were presently humming about the heads of Ben and his brother. Ben groaned with unwilling admiration of such marksmanship.

He was glad when they passed the ragged rock jaws of the ravine's entrance. They would not be able to get to the height above, into the shelter of the bad lands, but somewhere in the narrows of the ravine they might be able to put up a last fight. And—well, it was best not to think too far ahead.

Into the ravine behind them swept the uproar of the shouting man hunt. It seemed clear to Ben Trainor, now, that this was the end. And then, above him, from the edge of the right-hand cliff, he heard the clang of a rifle.

Who could be posted there to cut off their retreat?

He looked up and saw nothing. He glanced over his shoulder, and saw one of Christian's men dropping sidelong from the saddle. The other four were already in full flight, zigzagging their horses from side to side to upset the deadly aim of the rifleman on the cliff.

Ben Trainor, looking to the side, suddenly saw a rider appear on a golden horse, rushing down the dangerous slope to join that pair of hunted men.

CHAPTER XIV

The Rout

ALL fear left the desperate brain of Ben Trainor that instant. He had seen the rushing bore of a river, flooded suddenly by spring rains, and it seemed to him that the coming of Jim Silver was like that—a bright and powerful flood of rescue that would sweep all danger away.

Trainor turned, for he saw that Silver meant to go single-handed against those enemies, and Ben Trainor would not be left behind in the charge. Clive could shift for himself in the interim. But first of all the thought of driving into Christian and his allies was a wild joy to Trainor.

As he pulled his good horse about, he saw Clive slump weakly out of his saddle and collapse on the sand. Well, if all went well, they could return to Clive, but in the meantime Yates and Christian were to be handled. As he swung about, Ben Trainor saw that the man whom Silver's bullet had wounded had been picked up by two of his comrades. One of those rescuers was Perry. And perhaps it was because the wounded man occupied the attention of two of the party; perhaps it was simply because even men like Christian and Yates would not trust themselves in open fight, in spite of numbers, against Jim Silver—at any rate, the whole crew had turned and were fleeing as fast as their horses could go. And leading the retreat, with many glances over his shoulder, was the great Barry Christian!

A glory came over Ben Trainor as he shot his gelding away at full speed. He was hardly under way before the swift beat of hoofs caught up with him and passed him. The enormous stride of the golden horse, Parade, carried Silver off like a bird on wings. He gave one shout of greeting to Trainor, who saw the brown face of the wanderer set with a fierce resolution, and the eyes burning with savage hope.

Ben Trainor, as he vainly urged his horse in the pursuit, losing ground every instant behind Silver, knew why there was exultation in the soul of that famous man. For perhaps here, on this rim of the desert, the long pursuit of Christian was to come to an end. Here the long struggle might terminate.

Far back, as Trainor glanced over his shoulder, he saw the gray wolf, Frosty, running at full bent but hopelessly outdistanced by the speed of the horses. Parade and Silver would be the only ones of the trio present at the end of the hunt.

They rushed out of the mouth of the ravine, and there it was seen that Christian's party had separated. Even the fear and respect in which they held their leader could not induce these men to stand together and receive the shock of Silver with a united front. They fell away to this side and that. Off to the right rode the two who supported between them the wounded man. Straight ahead dashed Doc Yates. To the left the great Barry Christian was scurrying, flattening himself in terror over the pommel of his saddle, abandoning all shame in the presence of his most famous enemy.

So, it seemed to the excited mind of Ben Trainor, good has to triumph in the end. The crook succeeds for a little while, but before the close there is a day of accounting, a sudden rout and a downfall.

After Christian, like a hawk after a bird, sweeping with a strength and speed that made the limitless flat of the desert seem small, Parade drew rapidly farther and farther away.

Suddenly Trainor drew rein. He would never come up with the chase in time to be of use during the battle. And in the meantime, if he rode away, Yates and the others might decide to cut back and get at abandoned Clive Trainor, because of the priceless secret which was still locked behind the lips of the man.

So Ben Trainor halted his horse and strained his eyes until a cloud of dust grew up and made the wavering images thin, and finally they disappeared around a highland that projected well out from the main mass of the plateau.

After that, he turned back slowly, unwillingly. Over his shoulder he still saw Frosty legging it vainly after his master, the shaggy pelt humping in waves above his shoulders as he strained forward in the gallop. The tongue of the exhausted wolf hung like a red rag from his teeth, and he would never get to the scene in time to fight for his master.

Not a single one of the riders was now in sight, as Trainor rode back into the ravine. There he found that Clive had recovered enough strength to drag himself into the shadow of a rock. But the heat was very great. He panted continually, heavily. It seemed to Ben Trainor that each breath his brother drew might be the last one in his life.

That still, oven-hot air of the ravine would be the death of him, certainly, and one glance was enough to show that Clive could not be taken on to Alkali to find a doctor. Instead, the doctor would have to be brought to him. In the meantime, he must be put in a place where there was a greater stir of fresh air.

Clive was so far gone that when Ben offered a canteen of water at his lips, the older brother simply shook his head.

"I'm passing out," he said. "It's no good working over me. Get to Silver. Get him to help Nell. Don't waste time on me. I'm dying, Ben. I'm almost glad to die!"

He was sick with weakness and his wounds. The long ride had drained almost the last bit of his strength, and it was not strange that he was ready to give up the battle.

Ben Trainor said calmly: "What a cheap hound you'd be if you threw up the sponge while there's a drop of blood left in you or one beat left in your heart! Christian is being run down like a rabbit by Jim Silver. Yates is on the run, too. Perry has his hands full with a wounded man. We have our chance now to break through and win."

Clive Trainor groaned, as though the prospect of fighting his way back to life sickened him more than all else.

Then, lying back against the sand, he said: "I'm sorry I showed the white feather, Ben. But I'm tired. I'm damned tired. It seems as though the life's been running out of me for days. For weeks. Whatever life is in me is boiling out now. It's cooking out of me. Don't waste your time here. Back there at the old mine, there's only Blacky to keep an eye on Nell, and you say you've hurt Blacky badly. If you go straight back, you may have a chance to get her away from them. Don't think about me. Go to her, Ben."

"Perry and the rest are sure to go back past the mine," answered Ben Trainor. "Yates will be back there, too. As soon as they see that Silver has taken after Christian and is out of the way, they're certain to head for the mine. You can see that, can't you? My job is here with you. We'll climb up that side slip and get you up on the plateau where there's better air."

It was like handling a half-filled sack, whose weight continually threatened to slip through his hands, but finally Ben Trainor got his brother into the saddle, and walked beside the horse, steadying its burden, until they were up on the plateau again. There a single scrub of a tree offered shade, and Ben Trainor bedded down the wounded man there, while a slow stir of air instantly made breathing easier for Clive.

But it seemed that the life which Clive was so willing to give up was, in fact, rapidly leaking out of his body. Ben Trainor, caring for him, found more than one reason, and the broken statements of Clive pieced together the story of what had happened to him.

He had come to Alkali to try his fortune in the mines, but fortune, shortly after his arrival, had seemed to be hunting him out. A mere chance had brought him in contact with Nell Weston, newly in from the desert with a horrible story to tell.

She had gone with her father when that elderly man, broken in health and fortune, determined to try his luck prospecting through the barren hills near Mount Baldy. Luck and death came to him almost at the same instant. He had uncovered what he thought was a strike and he had drilled a hole and set a shot, but through a mistake in his clumsy operation, the explosion had occurred before he got to a safe distance. Weston was killed by the same blast which opened up a ledge of black rock in which there were bright yellow beadings that might be gold.

Out there in the desert, the girl had buried her father, and then she had come wearily into Alkali with some specimens of the ore. How to develop the mine she had not the slightest idea. She guessed that it would need capital, and how to raise capital she did not know. When she reached Alkali, she knew that the place was thronging with scoundrels, and, therefore, when she met and learned to trust Clive Trainor as an honest man, she gladly confided her problems to him.

The first thing he had done for her was to take a specimen of the ore to the assayer's office. Perhaps that was the first great mistake that brought on all the other evils in its train. No doubt the chief clerk in the assayer's office was in touch with Yates and the other crooks of Alkali. From that day forward, Clive Trainor had had a sense of being followed and watched.

However, the assayer's report was so staggeringly promising that he was inspired to invest his small capital to open up operations of the mine, on a small scale, at once.

He had bought drills, double jacks, powder, fuse, caps, provisions, four mules to carry the packs, and had hired three strong men to take over the major portion of the physical labor at the mine, all three representing themselves as experts. The other part of the story was revealed by the names of the trio, for they were the hired hangers-on of Doc Yates—Josh May, Cormack, and Blacky.

However, Clive Trainor suspected nothing. He felt it was a main point to get out of Alkali without being followed. The girl left in the late afternoon, riding out of Alkali in one direction. Clive Trainor went out after dark. Still later, Blacky and the other two left the town. The party of five assembled two miles outside of Alkali and went on through the night.

But trouble was in the air. Blacky was thoroughly drunk and could not speak without cursing so vilely that Clive Trainor had to speak to him sharply about it. That small thing started a quarrel, and Clive Trainor ordered Blacky to go back to the town. He was amazed by a downright refusal. When he told the other pair to speed Blacky on his way back, they laughed in his face. A moment later, Clive Trainor was a prisoner, tied to the stirrups of his horse, and the girl was likewise under guard.

That had not been the original plan of Yates, of

course. He had intended to let the girl and Clive show the way to the mine, which was hard to find. But at any rate, the thing was not taken seriously, because it was known that the girl had told Clive Trainor the exact location of the mine, and, therefore, the information could be beaten out of him. Blacky on the spot started the beating. But Clive stuck to his silence until he was knocked senseless.

He and the girl were taken up into the ravine where the old Spanish mine had been worked centuries before. That stone hut became a torture chamber for Clive Trainor. His body was reduced by every privation. Twice he was given no water for three days. Once he was hung up by the thumbs and a fire kindled under his feet, but he fainted so instantly, through the pain and his weakness, that they cut him down before he was seriously injured.

They tried the effect of a whip more than once. His body was half raw and covered with welts from those beatings. But still his iron endurance had held out until Christian, drawn into the difficult affair by the troubled Yates, finally suggested that the girl be tormented in the sight of Clive Trainor.

That crisis had been witnessed by Ben Trainor, of course. And the rest of the story he knew.

This tale from Clive Trainor did not come out smoothly, but in broken fragments which had to be pieced together by some guesswork on the part of Ben. But finally he had the thing clearly in his mind.

In the meantime, he had found a beggarly runlet of water a half mile from the spot—a mere trickle which disappeared among the rocks almost as soon as it lifted its head. There Ben filled the canteens again and again, making trips on the run in spite of his badly damaged feet. With that water he bathed the racked body of Clive and made him more comfortable.

It was all he could do, except wait for night and pray that strength would return to Clive so that in the cool of the night he could be taken back to Alkali. But in the mid-afternoon, Clive went out of his head with fever. He babbled, laughed, and chattered, or, turning his head from side to side, groaned heavily, deeply.

That day was a continued agony for Ben Trainor, who waited, praying for night or the return of Silver. And in the early dusk Silver came.

CHAPTER XV

Riding Parade

NEVER was a sight more welcome to human eyes than the picture of the rider of the great horse, with the slinking form of Frosty loping in front. They came up the ravine, and Frosty showed the way, at once, up the side slip where the Trainors had climbed to the top. But half the joy went out of Ben Trainor when he looked into the gloomy face of Jim Silver.

He had missed Christian again!

Doubling like a hunted fox into the broken bad lands of a long ravine, Christian had melted from view. Which one of half a hundred wandering little cross canyons the fugitive might have taken, Silver could not determine. Therefore, he had to wait until Frosty came up. And when the wolf came, he had to wait impatiently, until the keen nose of Frosty at last found the trail. After that, he was limited to the speed of the wolf in making the pursuit, and that speed, of course, could not match the striding horse that carried Christian. Finally, late in the afternoon, Silver had found that the trail led out from the highlands onto the desert, and there he had given up his man hunt.

"You gave it up to come back and see what was happening to Clive. Is that the reason?" asked Trainor seriously.

"There'll be another chance to get at Christian's trail," said Silver grimly.

He looked down at Clive, then knelt and felt his pulse for a long moment.

"He has to have a doctor," declared Silver, "and he's too weak to be taken to one. He needs careful nursing, anyway, to pull him through this. Trainor, I'll be the nurse. You ride to Alkali and get a doctor. Get the best one in the town. There are three of them. The best of the lot for talent is a drunken rascal called Wells. Better not try him, though. He drinks too much for his wits. Alexander is a good doctor. So is Murray. They're both Scotch and they're honest. The only fault with them is that they hate each other. Try to get one of the pair."

"I ought to stay here with Clive," said Trainor. "You'd do better with the bringing of the doctor, wouldn't you?"

"Your voice might quiet your brother," admitted Silver, "but he's beyond recognizing voices, just now."

Clive broke into long, delirious laughter, just then, and Silver laid his hand on the flushed brow of the sick man. The laughter died away. After a moment, Clive lay still, breathing hard and fast.

"What did you do?" whispered Ben Trainor.

"Animal magnetism—I don't know what it is," said Silver. "But it seems to help sick people. You go for the doctor. I'll take care of Clive well enough, I hope."

Ben Trainor argued no more, for he could see that his own care of Clive would be far less efficient than that which big Jim Silver could give. He merely saddled his horse, took a canteen of water, and mounted.

"They might come back to look for us," said Ben

Trainor. "And whatever they do, they're moving fast tonight. By tomorrow they know it will be almost too late to file a claim on their stolen mine and certainly after tomorrow, they know they'll be exposed. Tonight and tomorrow morning is about all the time that's left to them. They'll find a way of making the girl talk, tonight. They'll have the mine located before morning. They'll file the claim before tomorrow night, and once they file, the law won't let us shake them off."

"It depends," said Silver, "on whether the girl will hold out for a time or give in."

"A girl hold out—against Christian and Yates?" exclaimed Trainor.

"Your brother held out, and women are stronger than men," answered Silver.

"Do you mean that?" asked Trainor.

A deep groan began to tear the throat of Clive. The sound rippled through the very soul of Ben, but he heard it die away half uttered. The hand of Silver was again comforting the sick man, and relieving him with a hypnotic touch.

Silver said: "Women stand pain better than men do. Women make better martyrs. Maybe Christian and Yates will have their hands full before they make her talk. But whatever happens, you're to ride to Alkali. Go fast—take Parade and go fast!"

At the sound of his name, the great golden stallion came quickly toward his master, pricking up his ears.

"Ride Parade?" said Ben Trainor. "I know that nobody can ride Parade. No one except you."

"He'll carry you safely enough as soon as you know a few things about him and have an introduction," said Silver. "Come here, Parade." The horse came instantly up to him, and Silver laid his hand between the eyes of the chestnut.

"Put your hand under mine," he directed Trainor.

The instant Parade felt the touch of the stranger, his ears twitched back, he snorted and crouched a little. Trainor could feel, clearly, the shudder of revolt and of anger that ran through the great horse.

"Stroke his neck with your other hand; talk to him, Trainor. Get close to him and pat him like an old friend. As soon as he knows that you're a partner of mine, he'll carry you safely enough."

Trainor obeyed. It was not easy. Stroking the stallion and talking to him was something like handling a wild lion. He would not have been surprised, at any moment, if the chestnut had leaped away from the detaining touch of Silver and plunged at him with smashing hoofs and tearing teeth.

"It's no good," said Trainor. "I can't handle him. I can't make it. I'm afraid of him, and he knows it."

"He will obey you like a pet dog, in a moment," answered Silver, a little sternly. "It's not a question of fear. He's not afraid of anything, or of me. Do you think that I beat Parade or rode him into submission? No, no, Trainor. When a man takes a thing by force, he spoils it before he owns it. You'll always find that true. Parade and I became friends. That's all. Now you see he's stopped trembling. Now his ears come up. Get into the saddle, Ben."

Trainor, feeling cold with doubt and with fear, put his foot into the stirrup. He remembered the old tales of how this stallion had ranged the desert, wild, and gathered herds, and led them where men could not track him down until Jim Silver went out for weeks and months, and finally put the magic of his hands on the famous horse. More than a hundred thousand dollars, it was said, had been spent by one mustang hunter or another in the great effort to capture Parade, but only Silver had succeeded. And except for obedience to that one master, it was said that the stallion could be as savage as a mountain lion.

But now Trainor settled softly into the saddle, and felt the horse go down under him on tense springs, ready to hurl him at the sky. Gradually, as Silver talked, the tension relaxed. Parade stood alert, his ears once more pricking.

Silver stood back with a nod.

"There's only one danger now," he said, "and that's a danger to Parade. Because if you ask him to, he'll run his heart out and keep his ears forward and never say no to you, whatever you ask. Remember that. He'll face guns for you. He'll charge through a herd of enemies for you and fight his way with his teeth and his hoofs. But treat him well, and only use as much of him as you have to. Now you can start on."

"There's only a hackamore," said Trainor, still doubtful, though a little ashamed of his doubts.

"A touch will turn him," said Silver. "Don't doubt that. A word to him will do more than a spur. Good-by and good luck, Ben."

Ben Trainor turned the great horse. It was true that Parade obeyed a mere touch, though he tossed up his head and whinnied very softly to his master. Then, as though realizing that Silver would do nothing to stop this journey, Parade submitted and gave his attention to the difficult descent down the rocky slide to the level of the desert below.

He went like a mountain goat, daintily, swiftly, surely. His own self-training in the wilderness told, now, as he seemed to know by instinct which rock would endure his weight and which one was hung on an unsure balance. Lightly, rapidly, he ran a zigzag course to the level of the canyon floor and then strode away with a gait that made Trainor feel that he had been picked up by a strong wind and was being blown effortlessly forward.

Ben threw back his head. All that had to be done, all the danger of his entry into the town, all fear for his brother's safety or for that of blue-eyed Nell left him. The whole world went right, when a man sat on the back of Parade.

The hills walked rapidly past him. In the softer going of the desert sand, the stallion did not relax his striding. Out of the distance the lights of Alkali glittered, spread out wider from side to side. And suddenly Trainor remembered, conscious-stricken, that he had let the stallion run the entire distance at one mighty burst.

He drew rein, and heard the large labor of the lungs of the stallion and felt the thumping heart under his knee. Parade was dripping and shining with sweat. Another few miles at such a gait and he might, as Silver had warned, have run himself to death, but with a light stride and a swift one to the last moment of his strength. Trainor shook his head with shame and with pity. The rest of the way into town he walked Parade and loved and honored him with every step the horse made.

CHAPTER XVI

The Doctor

IN THAT same close grove of trees where he had tied his mustang the night before, Trainor now left Parade tethered, and patted the wet neck of the chestnut before he stepped out into danger.

Danger there would be, of course.

Before he found Doctor Murray or Doctor Alexander, it was very highly probable that he would be seen and recognized by one of the hangers-on of Yates, or a follower of Barry Christian. And the instant that he was known, there was sure to be a hue and cry raised after him. He had a revolver, which he was not very well able to use, and once more he would be confronting men who were born with weapons in their hands.

However, there was no purpose in waiting. He left the grove and walked up the side street. Before him sounded the hum of the town, and the lights of it were a dull yellow glow above the roofs, here and there, thrown up by the street lamps, or the big oil burners that flared above the saloons and dance halls along the main street. All of those sounds echoed through the mind of Trainor like gloomy warnings of a fate that might not be far away.

He stopped a half-drunken fellow who was coming down the street with uncertain steps. The man gripped Trainor's arm and steadied himself to answer the question.

"Murray or Alexander?" said the drunk. "Well, son, Murray won't be no more use to you in Alkali. You won't find him here."

"He's left town?" asked Trainor.

"He's up and left us all this afternoon."

"You don't know where he went?"

"No, sir, I don't know."

"Well, then there's Alexander. You know where his house is?"

"Yeah. I know."

"Tell me, then, will you?"

"Why, it's right up the street, there, two blocks. Got a high fence around it, so's you can't make a mistake."

"Thanks," said Trainor, starting to leave.

"Wait a minute. Alexander ain't in his house," said the drunk, pulling at Ben's arm.

"No? Where is he, then?"

"He's half-way," said the other.

"Half-way where?"

"To hell or heaven. I dunno which. Point is that him and Murray had it out this afternoon. He shot high and got Murray through the head, and that was all there was to that part of it. But Murray shot low and got Alexander through the stomach. And Alexander might live a coupla days. Will your sick friend last that long?"

"There's the other one, then," groaned Trainor. "There's Doctor Wells. D'you know where he is?"

"I know where he is," said the stranger, "but you wouldn't want him. He wouldn't be no good to you. Drunken fool, he is! Drunkenness is a terrible thing, partner. You wouldn't want to take no drunk doctor to a friend, would you?"

"I've got to have a doctor," said Trainor, "and I've got to have one soon. Will you tell me where I can look up Wells? Then I'll sashay along and find him."

"You that kind?" said the drunkard sadly. "You one of the kind that would take a drunk doctor to see a friend? Well, sir, then I don't want to know nothin' more of you, I don't want nothin' to do with you, and I ain't goin' to tell you where to find Doctor Wells."

"I want him for a friend that's drunk, too," said Trainor.

"Hey, do you?" exclaimed the stranger. "Well, doggone my rats, that's different. I could use Wells for that, myself. I gotta drink, partner. The doggone curse of my life is that I gotta weak stomach and I gotta drink to strengthen it up a lot. Y'understand, if you want a doctor for a drunk, Wells would be the best man in the world. He'd be the best man because he's the one that's done the most drinkin'. He's drunk now, up there in the back room of the Golden Hope."

That news struck Trainor in the face, heavily. He left his informant and went on slowly, knowing that it was no use to go ahead, but unable to turn back before he had at least looked over the situation. When he got to the rear of the Golden Hope, he could hear the music—a jigging of the violins, a blaring of muffled horns. And he was sickened a little, he knew not why, by the familiarity of the tune and the sweetness of the strings, and the terrible danger that waited for him in the place out of which that music issued.

Leaning back against the wall, he closed his eyes. To go in was death for him, he was reasonably sure; not to go in was death for his brother, who waited yonder, across the desert, with Jim Silver beside him.

He was no hero, Trainor told himself. Only men like Silver could rally themselves so as to go strongly and steadily ahead in the face of danger, loving duty more than they loved safety.

After a moment, he gathered his strength and did what he had done before—he pushed open the unlocked rear door of the place and stepped straight into the narrow hall which split the building into two parts. The same lamp gave him the same dim light.

He hesitated for an instant, but he knew, now, more about the layout of the place. Off to the left was the dance hall. To the right lay the main bar and the small rooms which were arranged behind it. He had been told that he was apt to find Doctor Wells drinking in one of the back rooms of the place, so he opened the first door to the right.

He found the place brightly lighted. A man in a checked flannel shirt, with the ends of a rusty-colored mustache showing past the sides of his cheeks, was seated with his back to the door, and facing him, looking straight into the eyes of Trainor, was the dance hall girl, Dolly.

The sight of her, the sense that he was lost and betrayed, stunned him, and then one of her eyelids fluttered. There was no other change in her expression—just that wink. He drew the door soundlessly shut and stood back in the dimness of the hallway, his brain whirling and his heart ill at ease.

The wink might have meant almost anything. But the fact that he had been seen was enough to drive him out of the place. Yet he could not go. He was still hesitant when the door jerked quickly open, and let into the hall a flash of brighter lamplight, and Dolly.

"Hey, bozo," said Dolly, "I'm glad to see you. What turned you to stone when you put an eye on me, a minute ago? Did you think I was going to sound the alarm, and whistle for the boys? I got rid of that mug who was in there with me. Now you can tell me what brand of hell-fire you're handling tonight?"

"I'm only looking for a doctor," said Trainor, "and—"

"Has somebody sunk lead into you, kid?" asked Dolly. "Are you hurt?"

She touched him with a swift, anxious hand.

"Somebody else is hurt and—"

"And you hurt 'em, and then you get soft and come for a doctor—wade right into a rattlesnake cave to get salve for the guy you socked and—"

"No, no," said Trainor, "the hurt man is—"

"And the boys in here are carrying a special kind of poison for you, brother," said Dolly. She put back her head and laughed at him, joyously, her eyes shining, her teeth flashing. "What a man you turned out to be, old-timer! Quiet-looking, too. Well, I always say that the quiet lads are the ones that make the ructions. That was a show you put on last night. I thought you were gone. I thought they'd polish you off, and when that yahoo of a barkeep came with his gun, did you slam him? Oh, you slammed him pretty, all right! But that was nothing; getting Blondy out of the soup was what counted."

"Why did you try that dirty trick on Blondy?" Trainor asked. "Why did you start doping him?"

"Oh, I ain't the Queen of Sheba," said the girl. "I gotta do what I'm told to do. When Doc Yates speaks, I gotta jump. But I was sorry for Blondy. I was sorry for the big red-faced ham. He was all right, today. He got out of town this morning, and he got fast. I guess Yates would have kept him here, but Yates was busy somewhere else. Blacky is back in town with a couple of yards of flannel wrapped around his bean. He don't smile when folks mention your name. He don't brag about the way he threw you out of the saloon. Look, kid. Being what you are, what made you let Blacky throw you out, that way? What made you kid him along like that? Were you fixing a harder spot to drop him in?"

Trainor would have been glad to tell her the truth, but he saw that she was not able to believe it. She wanted to create of him a master of the outlaw world, a desperate gunman. That was why she stepped closer to him, now, and laid her hands on his shoulders.

"You make a hit with me, Trainor," she said. "That mug of yours is what I call handsome. Open up and be nice, will you? Dolly isn't such a bad sort of a girl. Not to a fellow she likes."

"You're as game as they come, Dolly," he told her honestly. "Some day there'll be time for me to tell you a lot of other things. But go on and give me a hand, now. Tell me where I can get hold of Doctor Wells."

"The old souse is pie-eyed," said Dolly calmly. "He's up there in the next room, freezing onto a bottle and having a solitary drunk. That's the only kind he can afford to pay for, just now. He's blotto. He's no good for you, brother. I don't know where you shot the hombre that's sick now, but Wells wouldn't do him any good. He's mean when he's boiled. You couldn't do anything with him."

"Is he alone in that room?" asked Trainor.

"No. There's some others in there."

"Can you get him back into the next room, where you were before? That's empty now, isn't it?"

"I'll try to get him back. I'll try anything for you, Ben. When you pasted that barkeep on the mug, it was a personal favor you did for me, kid. Wait here till I open the door for you."

She left Trainor. A long minute followed, and still not a soul came down the hall. Then there was a tap on the door, and Trainor opened it and stepped through.

The girl was there, her arms akimbo, facing a great whale of a man with a fat, bloated face and eyes dulled and red-stained with alcohol. His mouth was loose. His whole body seemed loose with the effects of the poison. And yet there was in his face a suggestion of a strength which was still not entirely corrupted.

"Here, doctor," said the girl. "Here's an hombre that wants to see you and wants to see you bad. He's slammed a hole in the ribs of somebody and now he wants to get the hole patched up."

The doctor made a wide, but clumsy gesture of refusal.

"The whisky's too damn bad in this hang-out," he hotly declared. "Whisky ought to make a man steady on his pins, clear his brain, firm his touch. But this stuff is poison. I've got to spend some time with it. I'm going to analyze it, Dolly, and then I'm going to put the whole lot of you crooks behind the bars. Understand me? I'm going to put you behind. That's the job that keeps me here, and I'm not going to leave the place."

He kept shaking his head and waving his arm.

Trainor approached him.

"Keep away from me!" commanded the doctor. "I don't know you and I don't want to know you. I don't like you. You got a mean face. You got a bad eye. Get away from me. Dolly, where's that bottle of whisky?"

He turned toward the door of the next room, and Dolly made to Trainor a gesture of surrender. But Ben

Trainor could not be stopped so easily. He saw, now, that he had half a chance of winning the doctor to the purpose he wished, but it would only be through the means of a violent ruse.

He touched the doctor on the arm to stop him, at the same time asking Dolly to leave the room.

She went out laughing. "If you get Wells, you could get the King of England. Quick, Ben, or the crowd will find out that you're here, and then there will be the devil to pay for both of us!"

The doctor was very angry. He told Trainor to remove his hand at once. He told him that he was a boor and that under no conditions would the doctor do him any medical service.

Trainor cut that talking short by using the flat of his hand and striking Wells heavily across the face.

His hope was that the insult might sober the doctor a little. He was not prepared for the sudden and strong effect of the stroke. The doctor looked fixedly at him, lifted his hand, and wiped away a trickle of blood that ran down from his mouth.

"My friend," he said, "I'll have your life for this, one day."

"You can pay me back now," said Trainor, "if it will help to clear your brain at all. There you are, with your hands free."

Doctor Wells stepped right in with a hearty, chopping punch that clicked on the point of Trainor's undefended jaw and sent him reeling. Wells charged after him and was about to hit him again when he took note that the arms of Trainor were still hanging defenselessly at his sides and, therefore, he paused, puffing, raging.

"I'm going to thrash you, you puppy!" he said. "I'm going to teach you manners! I'm going to teach you that your elders may still be able to take care of themselves!"

"If you're sober enough to talk sense, then listen to

me," said Trainor. "If you're not, go on beating me till your brain is straight again."

Doctor Wells looked curiously from his clenched fist to the jaw of Trainor before he muttered words that Trainor could understand. Then he said, wiping his brow:

"Have I made a fool of myself again? Young man, who are you?"

"My name is Ben Trainor," said Ben Trainor.

"Great Scott!" gasped the doctor, retreating. "You mean that you're the desperado who—"

"My brother's almost a dying man across the desert," said Trainor. "He needs a doctor or he *will* die tomorrow. Fever, and weakness from starvation, and enough trouble to drive him mad. Doctor Wells, will you come away from town with me?"

However much alcohol was in the body of Wells, there was very little of it in his brain, by this time. He merely said:

"Trainor, whatever you may be, you're a brave devil for daring to come back into this town, and I'll go with you to hell and back, just as you say. I suppose you have your own way of sneaking out of Alkali. I'm going home to get a medical kit. I'll meet you on the road outside of town in fifteen minutes. The road toward Baldy."

He turned on his heel and went off briskly. Trainor, feeling that he had ended his main difficulty, and that he was on the verge of a complete success, opened the door into the hall just in time to see Blacky, Josh May, and two others come into the hall from the rear. He slammed the door in their faces, and threw the bolt across.

CHAPTER XVII

Man Hunters

THE wits went out of Trainor, in that emergency. The sudden yell that burst from the four scattered his thoughts as a wind scatters dust. A revolver bullet bored through the door and split it down a long panel.

Still he stood there like one hypnotized by the greatness of the terror.

He heard a rush of feet. The door, already cracked, burst open violently, with Josh May, who had been the point of the flying wedge, stumbling and then lurching forward on his face across the room. He fell right at Trainor's feet.

A bit of straight shooting would have finished off the rest of that charge in short order, but Trainor was still so benumbed in that brain that his hand did not seek the gun he so seldom carried. Instead, he picked up a chair, flung it into the midst of them, and leaped through the next doorway.

The noise and the gunfire had brought everyone out of the bar and swarming into the other back room, by this time. In the distance Trainor saw the twisted face of the bartender. But what counted was that the instant he appeared, the crowd fell back with a shattering yell of "Trainor!"

He might have laughed to think of the reputation which he had built up in this town. But he took that single instant of surprise to dodge through the mob, jerk open another door, and slam and lock it behind him. A bullet drilled through that door at the instant. But he had a second to decide which way he was to run—while that lock held behind him and the turmoil was on the farther side of the door.

To run to the rear was to plunge into certain danger. To go the other way might give him half a chance. So he ran forward, and through an open door into the long bar-room.

As he ran, he heard the ringing, familiar voice of Doc Yates, shouting:

"A thousand, five thousand for the scalp of Trainor! Get him, boys!"

Those words threw a sudden blackness over the eyes of Trainor. The last hope went out of him.

Here was the bar-room, empty for the instant, but with people in every room around it. Out on the street, men had heard the turmoil. Their footfalls beat heavily on the board sidewalk as they ran for the swing doors of the saloon. Escape seemed cut off in every way.

He vaulted over the bar and, as he dropped behind it, heard men rush into the room from the street, from two rear entrances.

And the voice of Doc Yates urged on the pack.

Trainor crept on hands and knees down the length of the bar, then turned into a little room behind it, where the walls were lined with shelves filled with bottles, while several big kegs stood on the floor. The window that gave onto the street was heavily shuttered on the inside and the shutters were padlocked.

He gripped those shutters, wrenched at them with all his might—and gained nothing. Twice his strength would not avail to tear them down. He needed a pry.

When he looked back, it seemed to him that the shouting, the thundering of feet had put the entire world in motion. His brain spun in the semi-darkness. He could neither think nor see, clearly, until he spied a heavy hammer lying on a shelf near the door.

He got to that hammer with a leap. It would serve him to pry open a board of the shutters; at the worst, he could use it to batter the shutters to pieces and so force an exit, if only he had time.

In the next room, the tremendous voice of Doc Yates was crying:

"Keep at it, boys! He's somewhere in this house. No chance for him to get out. He's lying low, somewhere. Five thousand to the fellow who gets him!"

That was what Trainor heard the last of as he snatched the hammer from the shelf and, swinging back toward the window, saw the twisted face of the barkeeper appear in the doorway.

Trainor struck. The weight of the hammer made the blow clumsy. It merely knocked the drawn revolver out of the hand of the barkeeper. The latter, disarmed, dived at Trainor like a football player and rolled him on the floor.

Still the bartender did not cry out. Perhaps the battle fury, perhaps the joy of finding his enemy here at hand had made the scarred man forget that a single cry would bring fifty men to his assistance. No, when Trainor got a glimpse of the face of the barkeeper, he saw the eyes gleaming with a cold and concentrated and alert malice.

Trainor could now understand. A yell for help would fill the room instantly with many men. It would also divide the promised reward into many fractions, and the barkeeper wanted the whole sum for himself. He had been disarmed of the revolver, but he had something almost better for hand-to-hand struggling—a bowie knife. Trainor managed to grip the wrist of the man's knife hand, and desperation froze his hold on it, and stiffened his arm to keep the point from the soft of his throat.

He could not maintain that resistance long. He was underneath. The weight of the barkeeper's whole body was bearing down to drive that knife home. Already the arm of Trainor was shuddering under the strain. The grin of triumph broadened horribly on the face of the barkeeper and kept his eyes glimmering.

There was no chance to help Trainor, then. Both his arms were occupied. Then he noticed that they lay close to the wall. He planted both feet against it and thrust out with all his might, with an impact that kicked them both over and over till their heads crashed against the rounded sides of one of the kegs.

Blackness jumped over the eyes of Trainor. As the flickering darkness came, he told himself that he was a dead man, with a knife in his throat.

Then instant sense came back to him.

The barkeeper was still striving, but the grin was frozen stupidly on his face; the strength was gone from his hand. With a twist, Trainor disarmed him. He heard the breath of the bartender caught, as he prepared to yell, and Trainor banged the rounded butt of the heavy knife against the temple of his man.

That one blow made the stunned man turn limp.

Trainor bounded to the shuttered window. There was still a rising tide of confusion thundering through the house. He could hear men upstairs, and in the barroom, and in the back rooms. There were footfalls and voices passing down the cellar stairs beneath.

And always there was that shout of Doc Yates which rang, trumpet-like, through the building:

"Five thousand for him, boys. You'll get him. Take your time, and be thorough. I'll have him if I have to clear the house and then burn it. Five thousand for the scalp of Ben Trainor!"

Trainor had fitted the handle of the hammer under the bottom slat of the shutters. He pried. The whole of the shutters trembled, sagged, gave way with a groaning of nail rust against old wood. He laid the hammer aside and with his bare hands wrenched the loosened weight away.

There was not even a pane of glass in the window frame. He had before him the dark of the night and the street not five feet below the window sill. One glance he threw over his shoulder, and then he slid through and stood on the ground, in the open air, free!

He slid in over the window sill half the length of his body, cupped his hands at his lips, and shouted with all his stentorian might:

"Doc Yates! If you want Trainor, come and get me, here! Come and get me, you blackleg! I'm here, waiting for you!"

That voice rang and re-rang and echoed through the building. It seemed to stun everyone to motionlessness, for an instant, but after that there was a savage rush of angry men, herding toward the point from which the cry had issued. Even from outside the building, the hunters were rushing back through the entrances, perhaps with some fine picture of a desperado standing his ground, ready to fight it out to the last against great Doc Yates.

That "desperado," the instant he had yelled, turned and fled with all his might down the street, and turned at the next corner, and again at the next, until he found himself utterly out of wind, but safe, among those saplings where Parade was tethered.

Then, through the darkness, he saw the glimmering eyes of the stallion. He spoke softly, and the great horse whinnied no louder than a whisper.

At that moment, it seemed to Trainor that there was no wonder that Silver could accomplish miracles, served as he was by even the dumb beasts.

He swung into the saddle. He rode quietly out into the narrow twisting lane, deep in muffling dust.

All across the town he heard hoofbeats, shoutings, and once there was a loud cluster of shots. But they would probably be shooting at every shadow, by this time. Men will do strange things for five thousand dollars!

He let Parade go into a trot.

Even the trot of the great stallion was smooth and easy, cushioned on the deep, supple play of the fetlock joints. And there was a springing speed to that effortless gait. It was at such a pace that a man should sit out a long pursuit, a long hunt, wearing down lesser creatures and mustangs which at full gallop could hardly match this travel gait of Parade. Yes, it was like being master of a wind which, at will, could be made to blow hard or soft, taking the rider out of the ken of lesser people.

He came beyond the town to the road to Mount Baldy. Down it he went for a mile, straining his eyes into the darkness. And there was no sight of the doctor!

Groaning, he stared about him. He should have known, he told himself, that the drunken doctor, half stimulated from his alcoholic state by an appeal to his pride and to his manhood, would quickly relapse as soon as the shock of the situation died down in him. He should have realized that ten minutes after making his promise, the doctor would be seated once more in front of his whisky bottle!

What could he do now? Return to a town that buzzed with rage and hate like a swarm of hornets? He had offended that great Doc Yates, to be sure, but he had also made a joke of all the grown men in Alkali. He wanted to laugh, as he thought of that, but he knew that the very birds of the air would see him on the darkest nights and cry out his name if he should so much as steal a pace back within the borders of the town.

He had failed, then, and the chance of saving Clive's life was gone.

Then, down the road from the town, at a steady, moderate trot, he heard the beat of a single horse traveling toward him. The shape loomed.

"Hi! Trainor!" called the loud voice of Doctor Wells.

CHAPTER XVIII

The Doctor's Decision

THE doctor had waited for a little while at the Golden Hope. He said that it was beyond human nature for him to leave and keep his appointment when the man with whom the appointment was made was being hunted up and down through the various rooms of the saloon. And then he realized, suddenly, that this was a challenge to his manhood. He ought to try to help. He ought to threaten Doc Yates with the law, and at least with the weight of his own hand.

Said the doctor: "And my hand was shaking like a feather in a wind. My heart was sick inside of me, sick and crazy. I was no good. I knew that if I jumped into a fight, I would accomplish nothing. I had to stand there and curse myself. And I cursed the whisky, too. I don't know, Trainor. It may be that I'll relapse into the old ways, but I hope not. I saw myself dead and lost and gone out of the world. I was alive, but buried. I was not a man, because the only life I led was the life of a dog. And while I was feeling that, I heard your voice come thundering, daring Doc Yates to come and face you!

"It was a shock to Doc Yates. He was there in a corner of the bar-room, shouting suggestions here and there, and when he heard you call, I saw him change color. He turned white.

"He had to go, or his reputation was damned, of course. But it took a moment to gather himself. I felt that I had to go, also, and that was where my nerve failed me. All that I could do was to follow along slowly on the out-

skirts of the crowd that jammed into the pantry room off
the bar. And there we could all see the barkeeper staggering about with big Doc Yates shaking him by the
shoulders and trying to get news out of him. When the
fellow could talk, he groaned out a few words about you,
and talked of a fight, and pointed to the open window.
Yates jumped right through the window. Half of the
others flooded after him. I heard two or three men say
outright if you'd gotten out of the Golden Hope under
conditions like those, you were the devil himself, and
they wanted no more to do with you on any trail whatever. And here I find you waiting for me, by thunder!"

The doctor began to laugh. "How did you do it, man?"
he asked.

"I had luck. That was all," said Trainor. "We've got to
get along. They may send hunters out over this trail. It's
a wonder that they haven't done it already. You have
brought your medical kit?"

"I've got everything with me, and a horse that will keep
up with yours. Lead the way."

Trainor led the way, and he kept to the long, smooth-
gaited trot with which Parade swept easily over the
ground until the doctor, his horse pounding along at a
steady gallop in the rear, shouted that the pace was killing off his horse. Then Trainor let Parade walk for a little
distance, while the doctor caught up. His horse was so
tired and blown that it stumbled repeatedly.

"Lacks exercise," said the doctor. "I've had the rascal
in good trim, though, when it could cover the ground
well enough to keep up with a buzzard in the sky. But
that's a fine horse you've got there."

Trainor laughed. "It's Parade!"

"Parade?" cried Doctor Wells. "You mean to say that
Jim Silver is mixed up in this?"

"He's with my brother now," answered Trainor.

"If you'd mentioned his name, you would have had no

trouble with me," answered Doctor Wells, "or with anyone who dares to call himself a right man. You would
have sobered me if you'd mentioned Jim Silver!"

In fact, that name seemed to blow the last of the
whisky fumes out of his head. He was a sober man entirely when they came up the narrows of the ravine, and
then climbed the difficult slope to the point where Clive
Trainor was lying. There Jim Silver rose from beside the
patient, and the muttering voice of Clive began to rattle
and rumble in delirium the moment the hand of Silver
was removed.

The big gray wolf stood bristling before the doctor until the word of his master sent him away. Parade, as
Trainor dismounted, went to snuff at Silver and then
tossed up his head like a happy colt.

"Very smooth work; very fast work!" said Silver to Ben
Trainor. He shook hands with Doctor Wells, who said:

"Whatever I can do, I'll do with all my heart, Silver."

Silver thanked him and stepped back with the younger
Trainor while the doctor made his examination.

"The other two are dead or dying," explained Trainor.
"I found Wells. He was drunk, but he sobered up a little,
and here he is! I don't think that there's much liquor in
his brain now. The ride seemed to get the alcohol out of
him—that and the mention of your name."

"Where did you find him?" asked Silver.

"In the Golden Hope. There was a bit of trouble, but I
got out of it without any bumps to speak of."

Silver looked quietly at him. He said nothing, but that
silent inspection told Trainor that he was being estimated
with new eyes. Then the voice of the doctor called to
them. The softness of gravity was in his words.

"He's been in hell," said the doctor, "and the marks
are still on him, as you know. He's been half-starved, and
that's weakened his resistance. He's been through such
things that he's suffering now from the shock. Bad shock.

Shock can kill a man just as easily and almost as quickly as bullets can. I simply want to tell you, Trainor, that I don't want to alarm you, but your brother is an extremely sick man. I've got some medicine that may get his fever down a little. I wouldn't try to move him in this condition. By morning he may be a lot better, or—"

Here he stopped and looked anxiously at the two of them.

The inference was very plain. By the morning, Clive might be much better, or he might be dead.

"Stay here with the doctor," said Silver. "I have something to do."

"I'm going with you," announced Ben Trainor. "If the doctor has the nerve to stay here alone, I'm going with you. The biggest thing that anyone can do for Clive is to finish the job that he laid out for himself."

"I'll stay here alone," answered Wells.

"Wait a moment," said Silver. "We've been spotted, not exactly here, but near here. It may be that they'll come back to look for us here. In that case, you'd be in a bad place."

"Who'd be doing the looking?" asked the doctor.

"Doc Yates and Barry Christian, with their men," said Silver, bringing out the words almost brutally.

The head of the doctor jerked under the impact of that news. He took a breath and then rubbed his knuckles across his forehead.

"Very well," he said at last. "I'll stay here. The two of you carry on. I know what's apt to happen if Yates and Christian come here together—but, after all, I like the gambling chance. I'll stay alone."

Silver nodded.

"Whatever we do, we have to wangle it tonight," he explained. "This is brave of you, Wells. We both appreciate it."

The sick man cried out in a sudden, high voice; the

doctor dropped at once to his knees beside him. He waved briefly at the other two, who stood waiting, reluctant to leave.

"Start out!" commanded Wells. "I'm going to wish you luck—and pray for a short night. But get on your way!"

CHAPTER XIX

Three Horsemen

A SEDATIVE, injected, made the locked and shuddering teeth of Clive Trainor relax. A fever potion was then worked past those teeth, and Doctor Wells, his forefinger constantly on the pulse of the sick man, finally leaned over and peered closely into the face. The forehead glistened with moonlight and with a small, fine sweat that was breaking through the skin. The breathing was deeper, slower. And the trembling pulse in the wrist began to throb more regularly.

The doctor sat back with a sigh which he was cautious not to make too loud. This man, for all he had been through, possessed a sound core of sturdy health that made his body respond swiftly to medication. An hour before, the doctor called it rather a bad gamble for Clive Trainor. Now he was certain that the man would get well. And he wondered, as he sat there and looked down at the calm face of the sleeper, how he, Wells, would have endured a similar strain.

He was rotten to the core with alcohol. It had made his body flabby. It had entered his mind like a decay.

He pulled out the fat flask he carried. There was a pint and a half of excellent whisky in that flask. He made a wry face, pulled out the cork, and let the dark stuff pour out on the rocks. It made a pool in a little hollow. He had a sudden desire to bend over and sup up the whisky from the pool. Instead, he stiffened his back and swallowed. His throat was dry.

Fear of the coming time racked him. He knew what it was for a man to swear off after drinking heavily for years. He knew the nervous quaking, the terrible tremors of body and soul, the ghastly illusions that beset the mind, and the vast hunger for the stuff gnawing in the stomach.

The doctor pulled out a handkerchief and mopped his forehead. He stared again at the wan face of Clive Trainor. He thought of the brother in Alkali. He thought of big, brown-faced Jim Silver, quiet and capable. No appetite was the master of those men!

And when he thought of this truth, a strength came up in him. He squared his shoulders, and looked away at the glimmering moonshine on Mount Baldy. He had been clean once and he could be clean again. He had been asleep, during these last years, and so he had sunk from depth to depth, sodden, until he wound up in Alkali, where a man like him need perform only one or two bits of work each week in order to keep drunk the rest of the time.

He made a gesture that washed away and abandoned that life. He set his jaw and shook his head. The shame of what he had been struck him in the face.

Then he heard, clearly, the trampling of horses that came swiftly up from the ravine beneath them. The doctor started to his feet, ready to call a welcome as Silver and Trainor drew in sight. Instead, he saw three strangers come over the ridge and ride up toward him.

"Better cover him, Bud," said one.

"All right, Perry," answered a second, and pulled from its long holster a rifle which he held at the ready, the muzzle toward the breast of the doctor.

This scene was to the doctor a great unreality. His eyes

perceived it, of course, but his reason said no to the images he beheld.

The third man, who wore a big bandage around his head, forcing his sombrero up high, the doctor recognized as the town bully and the bouncer of the Golden Hope—Blacky. All three had dismounted.

Blacky said, "Hello, doc. How's every little thing?" He spoke very casually, and then put his hands on his knees and, leaning over Trainor, murmured: "Here's the kid, again. I'll be doggoned if I didn't think he was rubbed so thin that he'd go all to pieces But he's sleepin' as sound as you please!"

The doctor said: "Stand back from him, Blacky. Don't disturb him. He's a mighty sick man and he needs this sleep."

"Yeah, does he?" answered Blacky. "What's the smell of whisky around here?"

"I poured out a flask," said the doctor calmly.

"You poured out a flask?" exclaimed Blacky. "The hell you did! By thunder, you did, too, and there's some of it caught in the holler of the rock!"

He dropped on his hands, smelled the liquid, and then sucked up the stuff greedily and noisily. He stood up, coughing.

"Mighty hot but mighty good," said Blacky. "First time I ever heard of you spillin' your drinks, doc. Damned if it ain't. Where you get this idea of pourin' things out?"

"Be quiet, Blacky," said Perry. "Listen to me, Wells. Jim Silver has been around here. Where's he gone?"

"I haven't seen him," lied the doctor smoothly.

"That's a lie," said Blacky cheerfully.

"It's the truth," insisted Wells.

"Who brought you out from town?" asked Perry.

"Ben Trainor brought me," said Wells.

"Yeah, he did, did he?" muttered Blacky. "He's a slick

kid, is that one. Maybe he's too damn slick for his own good, one of these days. You didn't see Silver?"

"No."

"Well, we got the kid, anyway," said Blacky.

"The chief's goin' to be glad of that," remarked Perry. "Tell the boys down below to bring up an extra hoss. We'll mount the kid and start him goin'."

"If you ride him in the saddle, you'll kill him," declared the doctor, exaggerating a good deal.

"Who cares if he bumps off?" demanded Blacky. "He's been nothin' but a flock of trouble, anyway."

"All you get out of any Trainor is a flock of trouble," declared the man called Bud.

"Wait a minute," said Perry. "You mean it would kill him, all right? You mean that, doc?"

"I mean that," said Wells.

"We'll make a stretcher for him," decided Perry.

Bud had gone to the edge of the plateau and was shouting down at the unseen men for them to bring up extra horses. By the murmur that answered, it appeared that a crowd was down there. But that was understandable. Men did not go hunting Jim Silver except when they were in numbers. Even then it was a task which most of them had wisdom enough to decline.

"Are you heeled?" Perry asked of the doctor.

"No," he answered, "I never carry a gun."

"Well, doc," said Perry, "I ain't even goin' to fan you to see if you tell the truth. But watch yourself. We're kind of in a hurry and we don't want to be bothered. You come along and keep your face shut, and maybe things'll be all right with you."

The doctor said nothing, and Perry, unshipping a small hand ax, which he carried behind the saddle on his mustang, attacked the straight branches of the tree. At the sound of the blows, Clive Trainor groaned, stirred, but did not waken, so deep was his exhaustion and so effective the sedative which Wells had injected.

Other men appeared over the ridge from the canyon, with led horses, and Bud took up an argument with Perry.

He said: "What you goin' to do, Perry? Load us all up with a lot of trouble? The chief didn't say anything about bringin' Clive Trainor in alive. He just wants his damned tongue fixed so's it can't waggle!"

"That's true," said Perry.

He stopped in his work, then added: "It ain't hardly human to leave him out here to die, though."

"Take the doc away from him, and he'll be done for by the morning," said Bud. He was a short, ape-faced man, and he talked with a great deal of decision and force. "We want to get this job done quick and turn back. That's what the chief wants us to do, and we'd better mind our step. Understand, Perry?"

"And the doc?" asked Perry.

"Oh," said Bud, "he'll keep his face shut. If he won't, maybe he'd better go with the kid, there."

"Look here, Wells," said Perry. "Will you keep your face shut about what might happen here?"

"If you murder young Trainor, do you mean?" said the doctor.

"You hear him talk?" muttered Perry to Bud. "He's goin' to blab everything he knows, when he gets back to town."

"Then don't let him get back," advised Bud.

"We can't wipe out the whole of everybody," declared Perry. "We'll let the chief pass on this. We'll take 'em both back to the boss."

"He'll give you hell for thanks," stated Bud. "Bang 'em both over the bean and let 'em lay, I'd say."

"There's Les, back there, shot through the middle," remembered Perry. "Poor old Les would be glad to see a doctor, I guess. And he might as well see this one. I've made up my mind. Come on, boys. Lend a hand, and we'll fix up a horse litter to pack this hombre along. The chief can do what he wants, but slammin' gents that are half dead already don't please me none too much."

The doctor, taking a very long and deep breath as he heard these remarks, examined the face of Bud, and saw the features twist and the teeth glint. The man was simply a beast, and his appetite was for blood. Even if the peril of that moment had been averted, Wells knew that there was more danger in the future, and that he would be lucky if he lived to see the dawn rise on this day.

He looked up at the sky, as even irreligious men will do when they have been relieved from a mortal peril. The moon shone very brightly, but off toward the northeast the lower stars were obscured by a mist. It was like a cloud that was rising out of the earth, not the heavens. The doctor was puzzled by it, not a little. The air was windless. A hush lay like a weight over the earth, and it was more than a little difficult to breathe. Yet in these conditions, which should have gone hard with Clive Trainor, he continued to sleep so profoundly that the doctor leaned and listened again to his breathing, and took his pulse.

Clive was much better, both in pulse and in respiration. The soporific was still working perfectly, and strength was flowing into that wasted body from sleep, like water flowing from a well into dry, dead ground.

In the meantime, the making of the stretcher was quickly completed, and two poles were tied into the stirrups of two horses. A blanket stretched across made the bed on which Trainor was laid. And even when he was lifted and put on the litter, he did not waken, nor when the horses were led stumbling down the steep slope to the level of the desert. He groaned faintly, once or twice, but nature was resolved on oblivion for the time being, and the sleep went on.

CHAPTER XX

The Treasure

IT WAS not long after that that Yates and Christian and three more rode out of the desert into one of those many ravines which cut into the edge of the upper plateau. The girl was with them, and she led the way to the head of the gulch. There she halted her horse and looked vaguely around her.

Christian suddenly joined her, caught the reins of her horse, and shook them angrily.

"This isn't the place!" he exclaimed. "The mine isn't here. My girl, if you're playing with us, you're going to remember tonight!"

She lifted her tired face to him as he spoke. Weariness takes the place of courage, sometimes, and she was very weary.

"You don't quite understand," she told him. "It may be that Clive has been taken away to safety by his brother. It may be that he's dead in the desert hours ago. But I've had to keep you occupied a little so that he could have a better chance of coming clear."

"Do you hear, Yates?" demanded Christian savagely.

"I hear," said Yates. "I told you that she was a tough little hombre, didn't I?"

"She may be tough, but she's going to be softened," answered Christian. "I'm going to soften her myself— and now."

He dropped the reins and grabbed the wrist of the girl.

"Are you going to take us where we want to go, or aren't you?" he shouted.

"My father died when that strike was made," she said to Christian. "Don't you think that he'd rather see me dead than have me be a guide to a pack of murderers and thieves?"

The steadiness of this voice made Christian stiffen in his saddle. Then he leaned and struck her across the mouth with the back of his gloved hand.

Her head jerked far back. One of the men yelled:

"Don't do that to the gal, Christian!"

Christian whirled his horse around with savage spurs and faced the speaker, with one hand on the butt of his revolver.

"Don't do it, eh?" cried Christian. "No, I'd rather do it to you, you fool! Are you talking up to me?"

"I'd rather have you do it to me than to her," said the fellow sullenly. "Damn it, Christian, she's a woman, after all."

"You're one of those chivalrous crooks, are you?" demanded Christian, forcing his dancing horse closer. "You'd shed your blood for the lady, would you? Why, if you open your mouth and speak another word, blood will be shed, and now!"

The other, tense, and bowed a little to be in readiness for action, endured the terrible eye of Christian only for another moment. Then his glance and his head fell a little. Christian made a contemptuous gesture of dismissal.

"Rats that squeak are not the rats that get the bait out of the trap," he said.

He jerked his horse savagely around toward the girl, again.

"I start now, with her," he said. "Yates, get off your horse and pull the fool out of the saddle, will you?"

There was no need to drag her. She dismounted quickly and stood with her hands clasped behind her, facing Christian who, on the back of his tall horse, looked like a giant. The man who had offered the first protest groaned a little, and turned his head away.

"You've brought this on yourself," said Christian. "You know that?"

"I know it," said the girl.

"I'm going to make you talk straight," said Christian, "and tear the truth out of you if I have to tear your heart in two at the same time."

"You've torn my heart in two already," said the girl.

"I've only scratched it," answered Christian. "I'm going to have you screaming, inside of ten seconds; screeching so that some of these milk-and-water fools will be pretty sick. I'm giving you your last chance to talk up. Will you do it?"

She looked straight at him, and then her head tilted back, and she looked far behind him. She said nothing.

"Hold on!" called an eager voice. It came from the same fellow who had turned away. "Someone's coming on the pelt. I know him. It's Perry. He's signaling. Here's Perry, and without his gang. What the devil could have happened?"

"Silver!" muttered another of the men. "They've run into Silver, and he's smashed 'em flat!"

"You lie," said Christian, his voice strained by fear. "It can't be that Silver has blundered onto them twice in a row. He can't have that much luck in a row."

Perry, swinging up rapidly, called out: "We've got Clive Trainor, chief. We're bringing him along."

The cry that came out of the girl's throat rang thin and high; it stopped in the middle of the note of terror and of grief. For Christian had begun to laugh.

"All the little chickens come home to rest. You see, Yates? I told you that the bad luck couldn't continue. Brains have to beat fortune, in the long run, and they're starting to beat it now! Well done, Perry! Well done, boy! You've brought luck back to us! I see 'em coming in now."

For the group which was coming at a walking pace, guarding the litter, was now in view around the corner of the ravine's wall.

"We found Doc Wells with him," said Perry. "Didn't know what to do with him, and so we brought him along, too."

"Why didn't you tap the drunken fool over the head and leave him there?" demanded Christian. "Nobody would have found him, and if they did, nobody would have cared."

"There was Les," said Perry. "Poor Les needs a doctor right bad, I guess."

"The devil with Les!" said Christian. "At a time like this, we can't afford to look behind us. Les is back at the shack, and he can stay there."

He turned to the girl again. "Here's your man again," he said. "Now, honey, are you talking with a straight tongue? Are you taking us out to the mine that the dear old father died for? Answer me, you white-faced fool!"

"I'll show you the way," said the girl slowly. "I give up —I give up if you'll let me have Clive safe!"

"Have him then," said Christian. "Get her back on her horse. Lead on, Nell. Be a little sprightly now. Get your horse into a gallop, and go fast. We've wasted most of the night, and it looks as though a sand storm may be blowing out of the northeast, yonder, to fill up the rest of our time! Go on! Go on! Right past 'em. You can see your man later on and mewl over him."

She put her horse to a good gallop and, in fact, rode straight past the group of riders, seeing among the horses the litter on which poor Clive Trainor was stretched.

Perhaps this last promise to her would be broken, as other promises had been broken in the past, but she dared not believe so. Out of the canyon she led the way and then angled off to the side a short distance into the desert.

Christian shouted to her: "You don't mean to say that you're fooling us again? There can't be a mine out here in the sand! You can't have made a strike out here!"

She halted her horse presently, and pointed at a small shadow that appeared in the moonlight, a mere head of dark stone that broke the watery surface of the moonlit sand.

"There!" she said. "And God forgive me! That's the strike!"

Christian leaped from his horse and knelt by the rock. He flashed the ray of a torch over it, but that was not necessary. The light of the moon was strong enough, and he found now, a great shattered place where an explosion had torn the soft, brittle rock apart. The whole face of the gash was glittering with a thin beadwork of gold, like that sample of ore which had come into the assayer's office in Alkali, not many weeks before.

Christian stood up, his face working. His eyes considered the men before him, and the others who were approaching from the distance, and he muttered:

"We've found it at last. We've found it! We've got it here!"

He laughed breathlessly. He turned to the girl and said: "I don't know why, but I can almost forgive you for being such a fool about young Trainor. You've brought us all to luck, at last. But there's no telling how far this runs. It may be only a boulder that's sunk here in the desert!"

"The blow sand has washed up over most of it," she answered. "Thirty or fifty yards of it were showing when I was here the last time."

"Out here in the desert, like a raft loaded with treasure on the open sea! There's something silly—there's something romantic about it! Look it over, boys! Look it over!"

The litter holding Clive Trainor had come up, by this time. Gusts of wind began to blow heavily. The cloud which Doctor Wells had seen in the northeast now covered half the stars, and in the air was an acrid smell of fine desert soil. Certainly the sand storm was growing on them rapidly.

Around that rock, heedless of the storm, the men of Yates and Christian were dancing, laughing. Some of them had found little shards of broken rock, and they waved these as drunkards might have brandished beakers of wine.

And then the heavy, sheer weight of the wind struck down on them all and blew the laughter away from their lips.

"It's coming!" shouted Christian.

He heard the girl appealing to the riders to turn back and take poor Clive Trainor into shelter among the ravines; otherwise, in his weakened condition, if he were left there, he would certainly be stifled under the thick blasts of the wind and sand. Even men and horses were sometimes overcome and choked by such a storm. Certainly an invalid would have but little chance.

"No!" thundered Christian. "I promised the girl that she could have her man. Where else would a man like to be? Put him down by the gold mine, and leave the girl with him. If the wind chokes him—why, that's too bad!" He laughed as he spoke. Then he added: "Give 'em a doctor, too. Let old Wells stay by 'em. He'll know how to help. Leave 'em stay here. Take the horses, and let 'em stay here and enjoy themselves with a gold mine for company! What more can they ask than that?"

It was done. Doctor Wells, standing, stupefied, looked into the face of the increasing wind until the flying sand began to sting his skin. When he turned, he found himself alone with the two helpless victims, and far away, the troop of riders were retreating into the mouth of a ravine which Doc Yates had said, "had walls so high and tight that not even a fly could crawl out of it, and, therefore, damned little wind would get in." Then Wells looked down at the girl, who lay weeping beside the litter of Clive Trainor. And only now the sick man commenced to waken.

CHAPTER XXI

The Dying Man

FAR up the long ravine, through the narrows, up the hill of loose sand, Jim Silver and Ben Trainor had come close to the stone house in front of the old Spanish mine. For here, they hoped, they might be able to pick up the lost sign of Barry Christian's men. Leading the way was Jim Silver's tame wolf, and when Frosty came to the black, open doorway of the house, he suddenly shrank down and leaped aside. He began to back toward his master with his head down, his legs bent so that he was in a position to leap in any direction.

The horses had been left at a little distance, and now Silver murmured to Trainor: "There's a man in that house. Take the back. I'll take the front. Frosty wouldn't act that way except for a man and guns."

"There may be ten men, for that matter, and the darkness may be only a bait," said Trainor.

"No," answered Silver. "If there were a lot of men, Frosty wouldn't come back slowly. He'd come on the run. Take the back way; I'll take the front, and we'll see what's inside the place."

Trainor, in fact, had barely skirted to the rear of the

house when he heard Silver say, from the front and inside:

"Steady, brother! Don't move! I see you in spite of the dark."

"Move?" answered a groaning voice. "The only place I can move to is hell, and I'm bound there pretty fast."

By the time Trainor got in, Silver had already kindled a lantern and with Trainor he looked down into the face of a man who had a great red-stained bandage about his body, which was naked above the hips. A blanket had been thrown on the long table, and that one of Yates's companions who was called Les was stretched there to die or live, as chance might help him or leave him.

He was a good-looking fellow in his early twenties, with a growth of pale blond stubble over his face. His brows were puckered with pain that made him turn his head restlessly, continually, from side to side. But when he saw Silver, his head stopped its turning, and his eyes fixed.

"It's a funny damn thing," said Les. "I kind of thought that I'd see you again. And here you are, eh? Well, you got me, Silver, and I guess you got me good. Either of you hombres would kindly please to gimme a slug of water out of the canteen over yonder? I can't get down off the table to fetch it for myself."

Silver brought him the canteen quickly and held it at his lips. Les drank with bulging eyes.

"That's better by a whole lot," he declared, panting. "Luck that brung you two here—luck or that devil of a Frosty, eh?"

For the wolf had reared and, planting his forefeet on the edge of the table, lolled the long red flag of his tongue and looked with green eyes into the face of the wounded man.

"Frosty brought us," said Silver, "and told us that there was someone in here in the dark. Where are the rest of your pals, Les?"

"Dead, I hope!" said Les. "They go off and leave me here to die! They wouldn't fetch me a doctor. They wouldn't leave one man to look after me! Perry wanted to. And Christian he just cussed Perry out. Perry's a white man, but Christian's a snake. What does he care if I live or I die? 'We got no time to pick up the hindmost' is all he says. And so—"

He began to cough. With both hands he grappled the pain in the center of his body. His mouth opened. The coughing stopped, but the convulsion of it remained on his face.

"Don't talk any more," said Silver. "I'm sorry you're hurt, partner. We'll fix you a decent bed, before we start. And then—"

His voice died out, for a crimson froth came bubbling on the lips of Les, the telltale sign that he had been wounded through the lungs. Les wiped his lips and looked at the froth on the back of his hand. Then his staring eyes gaped at the two.

"I'm goin' to die," he whispered. "Whatcha think of that? I feel right strong, but I'm goin' to die!"

"You may not," said Silver. "Lie still. Be quiet. We'll —we'll stay with you—one of us will!"

"Will you?" muttered Les. "No, don't you do it. I'm goin' to go quick—there ain't much air—I can't get hold of no air. Don't stay here with me. Go and get on the trail of Christian and blast the heart out of his body. Go and open him up! I'll tell you where to look. The girl led 'em over to Slocum's Ravine. The one with the walls stickin' straight up on each side. It's a gulch that not even a fly could climb out of. She said that that's where the mine is. You'll find 'em there. Find 'em and shoot to kill. They all oughta die, the skunks! Only Perry is kind of a white man. The rest had oughta die! Go get 'em, Silver!"

He lay still, panting, and his eyes rolled rapidly in his

head. His mouth opened and shut as he bit at the air.

Trainor looked with horrified inquiry at Silver and received one quick glance that said, "No!"

"As long as I had to be bumped off, it was better that a gent like Silver should do the trick," said the husky whisper of Les. "I sort of wish that I'd been on your side of the fence, Silver, and gone straight. I ain't been a lazy, crooked hound like a lot of 'em—more kind of crazy and didn't care. And now, I'm finished up. They ain't goin' to forget me, just because I'm on your list! But if only that bullet had socked into Christian instead of me! It might've, just as good! The world would be a lot better off. Wouldn't it?"

He twisted again, from side to side.

"Is the pain bad?" said Silver.

"Yeah, bad, bad!" gasped Les.

Silver laid his big, brown hands softly over the bandage. Les suddenly let his own hands drop away.

"The pain," he said, "it sort of goes right out—into your hands—like it was running out into them!"

Like a child, he wondered at Silver.

"This ain't so bad," said Les. "This feels pretty good. If only I could breathe better. Silver, am I goin' to die?"

"You're going to die, Les," said Silver. "I'm sorry."

"Would you be sorry, honest?" asked Les.

"With my whole heart, I'm sorry," said Silver.

"You're a good guy, Silver," whispered Les. "Yeah, and we all of us know that. Even Yates and Christian know it. We all know that you're the right sort. Only—we fought against you. I'm sorry for that."

Suddenly he went limp. His lips moved. No words came.

"Silver!" he called out suddenly and sat straight up. Silver caught him in his arms. The head of the dead man fell back against his shoulder.

Ben Trainor looked not at the dead face, but into the

sorrowful eyes of Jim Silver, as the big man lowered the body gently onto the flat of the table, again. He pulled the blanket over the head of Les after he had closed the eyes.

"That's that!" he said. "We ride for Slocum's Ravine now, and try to make up for this mistake of mine, Ben."

CHAPTER XXII

The Storm

THE unhampered stride of the golden stallion would have brought Silver to the mouth of Slocum's Ravine in time to interfere with the retreat of Christian and his men as the sand storm blew up, but Parade had to be checked to keep back with the gait of the horse of Ben Trainor. That was why, from the distance, the two riders saw the rout of mounted men pouring into the narrow mouth of the ravine on whose polished sides the moon was still glimmering, though across the desert, rapidly enveloping Silver and Trainor, the sand storm was increasing in strength and in darkness.

"It's no good!" shouted Trainor to Silver. "We've got to get to some kind of shelter and—"

"Look!" said Silver, calling through the bandanna which he had tied across his face to shut out the flying dust. "We've got to get to those people and see who they are. Two of 'em, left out there—why do the fools stay? Do they think that they can get shelter from that bit of rock? Or is it some of Christian's devilishness? Trainor, those are his men who just went back into the ravine. I've half a mind to ride in behind them and—"

A sudden, howling blast of the wind cut short these words. The two men went forward to the figures which were now barely distinguishable as they strove to take shelter behind the rock.

The moon was gone. The sheeted dust made a false twilight as thick as the last hour of dusk, and through it the two men forced their horses.

Trainor, as he reached the goal, saw the girl trying to make more shelter for a helpless man stretched flat on his back; through the murk, he thought he could make out the face of his brother, and he threw himself hastily from the saddle.

It was an almost fatal error, as time was to tell, for the horse, wild with fear in the storm, snatched the reins through the fingers of Trainor and suddenly bolted before the wind. Only for an instant was it visible, making gigantic strides as though the wind were buoying it up on wings. Then it was gone.

Trainor, for the instant, paid little heed to that. He was sprawling flat, helping to make a shelter for his brother. Silver was there, also. On the flat top of the gold rock, he had made Parade lie down, thereby increasing the height of the barrier toward the wind. Under the lee of that shelter the five people huddled.

Speech was impossible. The wind screamed like a thousand fiends. The heavy body of Parade, even, was shaken and battered by its force. And in the thick murk of the night, Ben Trainor could barely make out what was happening close beside him.

Clive, happily, was bearing the thing fairly well. That was because Silver took charge and from the first carefully moistened the cloth that covered the face of the sick man. That moisture helped to strain out the incredibly fine sand which was sifting through the clothes of the others. It not only worked in up sleeves and down neckbands, but also it actually blew right through the strong fabric of the cloth! Wherever the air could penetrate, the fine sand could work with it!

Ben Trainor and Wells and the girl, huddling over Clive, helped make the barrier more solid against the sweep of the wind, but that was all they could do. The fight to keep breathing was enough to tax them. The frightful sense of stifling drove Ben Trainor half mad. He wondered how the girl could endure. And yet she offered no complaint, by any gesture. Neither did Doctor Wells. However, it was Silver who did everything. It was he who busily pushed away the sand that whipped around the rock like water. The moment that it was thrust out, as it threatened to overwhelm the group, the wind caught hold of it and knocked it into a cloud that traveled off with a hissing sound down the wind. It was Silver, too, who continually turned and swabbed out the nostrils of Parade. Sometimes, in a lull of the wind, he reached into the mouth of the stallion and, with a few drops of water on a rag, swabbed out the dust that was clogging the air passages of the nose, making the mouth dry. The same service he performed for Frosty, who lay, as a rule, with his head thrust under the coat of his master.

The magic hands of Silver were nearly always busy, with the two animals, and with the sick man. And now and then he bowed his head and listened to the heartbeat of Clive Trainor. For it might well be that the suggestion of Christian would come into effect, and that Clive would stifle in the storm.

One thing was certain—they could not move either with the storm or against it. The weight of the wind was such that even a horse could hardly have stood in it.

And this continued for hours.

Doctor Wells had begun to act strangely before the end of the strain. Ben Trainor could see the medical man swaying his head and then his entire body from side to side, as though he were in great distress. But he was not prepared to see Wells suddenly leap to his feet with a gasping cry, that sounded faint and small and far away.

The wind, as he jumped up, took him with many hands and jerked him away. He rolled helplessly in the sand, and it was Silver who sprang after him—Silver and Frosty!

Ben Trainor, stunned, had barely begun to rise to give his hand, when already he saw the doctor dragged back by Silver, who leaned with his body almost horizontal, and with Frosty backing up, tugging with all his might at the coat of Wells.

The doctor was unconscious.

No doubt he had been gradually stifling for a long time, fighting to keep himself calm while the sand coated the inside of his nose and mouth, even through the doubled folds of his bandanna. The shattered nerves and the alcohol-weakened heart had endured this long simply because the will of the doctor had bravely held on. But at last, in a panic, all had given way together. He had leaped, in the throes of strangulation, to his feet, and had been hurled into the darkness by the stroke of the wind.

Now, his nose and mouth filled with sand—blind with it, also—he lay like one dead while Silver worked over him. More of the precious water had to be used to swab out the nose passages. Water had to be poured down the throat of the senseless man. It seemed to Ben Trainor that poor Wells was surely dead. And then, by the grace of Silver and good chance, the man began to move. It was merely a movement of the hand, but it announced life.

And just after that the wind began to fall away.

Its terrible screaming dropped down the scale several notes at a time. It was possible to uncover the eyes, if they were carefully squinted. And as the wind fell away, the masses of the flying dust diminished. The light of the moon once more was filtering through, and the group could look about into each other's ghastly faces.

They were winning. They had two helpless men on their hands, but they were winning—for the moment.

What would happen when the storm had passed quite on and the men of Christian rode out again? They would find the group huddled up, waiting for destruction.

It was possible even now to rise and walk against the wind, barely possible. But even if both the helpless men were put on Parade, the other three would have to remain on foot, and they could not travel a mile before the savage horsemen of Christian would bear down upon them.

They had this moment while the wind screamed less fiercely to make up their minds.

Wells was badly done in. Silver, taking his heartbeat, shook his head gloomily. The honest doctor had endured, as a matter of fact, too long. He should have asked for help before coming to the verge of prostration. Now there was the very effect of shock which he had noted in Clive Trainor.

Whatever was done, Wells would have to be considered a helpless weight of flesh.

As for Clive, he was alive; perhaps it would be better for him directly, but he was very far gone, and as the wind fell, Ben Trainor could hear him muttering rapidly, somewhat vaguely, without meaning. The delirium, it seemed, had commenced again in him, and no wonder!

The girl?

As the falling of the wind, and the hurtling mists of dust made it possible for her to uncover her face, it appeared like the faces of the others—black as a Negro's, because the covering and the heat had produced rivers of sweat that turned into rivers of sticky mud. But she actually seemed less affected by the storm than any of the others. Perhaps that was because she had had the head of Clive Trainor in her lap all through the crisis, and her hands had cherished him, following the precepts that Silver showed her.

Silver himself? The storm seemed to have passed over him as over a rock. He was busy, now, caring for the stallion, which was snorting the clotted dust out of its flaring nostrils. Parade, no doubt, had saved them more than all else, with the bulwark of his body.

Then Silver called loudly, through the dying yell of the wind: "Ben, what are you thinking of?"

Ben Trainor had been thinking, and not in vain.

"That ravine—you remember Les said that not even a fly could climb out of it?"

"Yes, I remember."

"Then suppose that a man with a rifle and plenty of ammunition lay right in the mouth of the gulch and opened up on anyone who tried to get out? Wouldn't that plug the valley like a cork in a bottle? Wouldn't that hold 'em all there until help comes from Alkali?"

Before he got an answer, Ben Trainor added: "But we'll get no help out of that town. I forgot that!"

"We'll get plenty of help," said Silver. "Don't think that everybody in Alkali is a crook. Not a bit! With Yates and Christian gone, we can get plenty of followers— enough to ring that valley around, I tell you! Trainor, go back with the others. Parade will carry Wells and Clive. Nell and you can walk. I'll stay here and bottle up the valley."

"No," said Ben Trainor, though the heart in him shrank as he spoke and saw the danger that he would have to face. "You'll have to go with them to handle Parade. How could I make him carry double? And there's no time for you to teach him; Christian's rats may poke their heads out of the hole any minute now. Besides, it's Jim Silver that will raise the crowd in town. What could

I do? Nothing! But even the crooks will follow Jim Silver! It's your job to go!"

He knew that he had spoken the truth and the full truth. Even Silver was silent, though his face worked as he peered through the flying mist of dust toward the mouth of the valley—where his heart was urging him to go. For in there was Christian.

Ben Trainor gripped the senseless hand of his brother. He patted Wells on the shoulder and drew a feeble groan for an answer.

The hand of Silver almost crushed Trainor's, and Silver's own rifle was passed into his hands. They said nothing. They merely looked at one another.

Then the girl stood up. The wind staggered her, and she gripped both hands of Ben Trainor, and let him go, head down, blundering, stumbling, toward his post of danger and honor.

CHAPTER XXIII

In the Trap

BEN TRAINOR got there in time. He lay in between two rocks that stood like reefs in the whitening river of sand that flowed through the throat of the ravine. As he stretched out there, he could see the dust haze clearing away and the moonlight beginning to glimmer more and more brightly on the polished walls of Slocum's Ravine, up which even a fly could not walk. Not very high walls, but high enough, he told himself.

There was grit between his teeth, grit down his back, crawling grit that irritated his flesh, and grit that half blinded his eyes. But he was blinking them clearer and clearer. And there was plenty of moonlight. There was enough to show him the huddle of shadows at the farther end of the ravine which had sheltered Christian's party from the sand storm, but had not sheltered it enough. The huddle of shadows was rising from the low rocks that were spilled about the floor of the little valley, and Trainor could see everything. He could see everything except the little cones of security which existed behind the rocks, here and there.

The moon lay in the west, but before it went down, the sun would be up, to give better shooting light than ever. And at about the same time Jim Silver would come back from Alkali with many men. They would clean up the whole lot of bad men inside. They would sweep up the entire gang, and in that gang was the man most infamous—Barry Christian! When Ben Trainor thought again of the pale, handsome face, the magnificently towering forehead, and that cold smile of Christian, he knew that the man represented all the evil that could be gathered in one human being, and he was glad he was there, closing the mouth of the trap with his rifle. He liked the job. He had no love of bloodshed, but he could shoot into these scoundrels with as free a conscience as ever a hungry man had when he killed for venison.

The wind was falling rapidly. There was still flying dust in the air, but it diminished constantly and let the strength of the moon come through. And everything was perfect. Ben could see the entire inside of the gulch. All was spread out before him. He had plenty of ammunition, and he had Jim Silver's own rifle. To be sure, he was no great marksman, but he could not very well miss a target as big as a man at these ranges. So the savage that is locked up in the breast of every man grew great and heated the blood of Ben Trainor.

Christian's men were preparing to move. The horses were being mounted. A tall, imposing figure rode first toward the mouth of the valley. That was Doc Yates.

Trainor glanced once over his shoulder. He could see, dim and small with distance, a crawling cluster of life that moved slowly away toward the Alkali trail.

Then he looked back toward Yates, and leveled his rifle. It would be easy to pick the man off. He could drill him through the breast, a little to the left of center and half-way down between shoulder and hip. That would get the heart. Or else he could take him through the head. That would be easy, too, and he knew it as he steadied the gun. The fact that it had belonged to Silver made him feel, somehow, that it could not miss. But it was hard to shoot a man from ambush, without warning.

Instead, he put a bullet a few dangerous inches away from the head of Yates, and saw the fellow duck so violently that he almost fell out of the saddle.

Yates turned his horse around and fled, flattening himself along the back of the animal. But he could not flee far—there were the walls of that ravine which even a fly could not climb, and they would hold Yates and all of the others, safely.

Trainor fired again, sending the bullet once more over the heads of the thickest cluster. And as turtles dive off low rocks, scuttling into the water, so those men of Christian dived out of their saddles and took shelter here and there behind the meager stones that dotted the bottom of the ravine.

A gust of rifle fire came at once. They had located the site of Trainor's post. Now they pelted and swept it with lead. He heard the brief whining of the bullets. He heard and even felt the shock of the pellets against the stones that shielded him.

So he lay low, head down, taking it easy. They could shoot like that till doomsday, without being able to budge him or break down his defenses.

Then he heard the beating of hoofs.

He ventured a glance and saw three riders sweeping

at full gallop toward the mouth of the ravine. The tactics were simple and they might be effective. If Trainor's rocks were sufficiently blanketed with gunfire, he would not be able to show himself to shoot.

Even that slight lifting of the head had let him fairly feel the breath of a bullet passing his cheek.

He got the rifle ready. He would have to take chances —but it would surely be the end for at least one of the three who were charging. He only wished that Yates or Christian were among the trio!

Up with the rifle—a quick shot at point-blank range just as the three neared the mouth of the gulley, and the central rider toppled and dropped over to the side. His companions on either side pulled up their horses with yells of rage and fear. A shout of dismay came from the remnants of the gang in the rear. They could not maintain such a fire, now. Their own men were a screen, in part, between them and Trainor.

To right and left the two unharmed riders jerked their horses. The stricken man kept on falling. He hit the ground, and a puff of dust rose from the spot, like an explosion. He trailed, his foot caught for an instant in the stirrup. Then the mustang broke free and raced off into the desert, not three yards from Trainor's nest in the rocks.

After that came a fiercely concentrated burst of rifle fire. The air was thick with the wasp noises. It died out, and Trainor heard, close to him and in front, the groaning of a man sick with pain. That was his victim, lying out there beyond the reach of his friends, lost.

The rifle fire had ended when the voice of Perry shouted, fairly close to the entrance of the gulch:

"Who's there? Who's there? Is it Jim Silver?"

Trainor laughed silently. If he held his tongue, they could keep on imagining it to be Jim Silver, and that would more effectively bottle up the ravine than any rifle work. They would take no chances in face of the gun of terrible Jim Silver!

"Listen, Silver!" called Perry. "Let us take Chuck back inside, won't you? He's dyin' out there. It don't do you no good to leave him there. Will you let us take him back inside?"

Trainor made no answer.

And the groaning voice of "Chuck" appealed to him: "Silver, you was always a white man. You never was a low skunk like the rest of us. Leave me have a chance to get a whack at a canteen, will you? Gimme a chance to have one drink, will you, Silver?"

"All right!" said Trainor. "Come out and take him in. I won't shoot."

"It's Trainor!" he heard Perry exclaim.

And then there was an outburst of rage and hate from many voices.

"Come on, Blacky," urged Perry. "Gimme a hand to get Chuck back inside, will you?"

"Not me," shouted Blacky. "I won't show myself. The kid couldn't help plugging me if he got the chance."

"He won't double-cross you. He's a white man," said Perry. "You come along with me, then, Lem."

Two sets of footsteps came toward the rock of Trainor. He did not show himself, for the thing might be a blind —this rescue, this act of humanity only arranged so that cunning marksmen, their rifles on the target, might slip lead into him the instant he lifted up.

"Let me hear you moving about, boys," said Trainor. "Don't try to sneak up on me, is all I advise you."

"We won't try to sneak up," said Perry. "It's white of you to let us take poor Chuck in. It's damn white of you, seeing what we've been doing."

"I'll go one bigger step for you, Perry," said Trainor. "You can walk right past me and keep on walking. You're free to go, if you'll drop your guns before you start. You're not like the rest of this poison."

"Thanks," said Perry. "I've throwed in with these hombres, and I guess I'll stick with them to the finish. You know how it is, Trainor, I made my bed, and I'm goin' to lie on it. I ain't goin' to walk out on them when the pinch comes."

Trainor could hear them moving away; he could hear the diminishing groans of the wounded man, cursing those who bore him, damning them for the cruel strength of their hands, which tormented him.

Then another voice spoke from near the mouth of the ravine, and it was Barry Christian.

"You hear me, Trainor?" he asked.

"I hear you, yes."

"I want to talk business with you."

"You can't talk to me, Christian."

"Every man will listen to business. So will you, Trainor. Listen to me. I'm not talking small stuff. I'm talking big."

"Go on. How big?" asked Trainor.

"Ten thousand dollars. Not a promise. I've got the cash for you, here and now."

"It's a lot of money," said Trainor. "But it's not enough."

"Think it over," said Christian. "Ten thousand is a big pile. It will take care of you the rest of your life, if you invest it right and do a little honest work besides. Ten thousand—more than the savings of a whole lifetime."

"It's a lot, but it's not enough," said Trainor.

"You want to remember," said Christian, "that you'll be protected. We'll fix up the escape so that it'll look perfectly natural. It'll seem that we managed to get out and surprise you—we'll leave you tied hand and foot, if you want us to. Nobody in the world will ever be able to suspect that you sold out. We'll fix it any way you want."

"Thanks," said Trainor, "but you haven't hit my price yet."

"All right," said Christian. "You boost the figure, then, and tell me what you want. If I haven't got it in cash, I'll give myself into your keeping, until my men bring you whatever you want."

"You can pay my price without money," said Trainor. "There's a point of rock that juts out, down there in the ravine. Let me see a couple of ropes strung over that rock. Let me see Doc Yates hanging from one end, and you from the other—and I'll let the rest of the boys go scotfree."

He heard a snarl of rage from Christian. Half a dozen rifles exploded in one heavy clap of thunder. And that was the end of the parley.

He waited. Once he ventured to look out around the edge of the rock, and he saw the horses coming into a single cluster, apparently of their own volition. A rifle bullet dug up sand and threw it into his face as he risked this glance.

He lay back to wonder what device was now in progress in the fertile brain of Barry Christian.

CHAPTER XXIV

Ropes to Freedom

TRAINOR could only venture a spying glance now and again. Then he saw that the horses were being collected, without the hand of a man showing, because ropes had been flung over their heads, and in this manner they were drawn about until they were ranged in a compact line, a dozen of them. Then a voice sang out:

"Are you ready, boys?"

From closer to the mouth of the ravine the answer was: "Ready! Let her go!"

Then suddenly those horses were started with a wild yelling and whooping and a discharge of guns behind them. They came like mad, their bridles interlinked, and Trainor, with a shock, saw the intent.

The rifle fire doubled on his rocks, pelting this post all over with a close shower of bullets. And, in a moment, the solid wall of horses woud rush out of the mouth of the ravine. The instant that they passed it, behind them would come the men of Christian, sprinting. They would be so close to the rocks, by the time the horses passed, that Trainor would be unable to defend himself against the many-sided attack.

There was only one thing to do, and he hated that almost worse than shooting at a man.

He got a bead on the head of a horse in the center of the charging line, and dropped the poor brute with a bullet through the brain. Then the entangled bridle reins which were holding the horses in a solid line, making of them a perfect moving rampart, served to break up the charge instantly. The fall of the one mustang confused all the others and brought them up short as though on an anchor. Two or three of them tumbled head over heels. There was a great fighting and kicking among the horses. Then two or three of them broke loose and rushed singly out of the valley and across the desert. Others followed, drawn along as into a vacuum. The men of Christian vainly yelled and whooped and exploded guns near the mouth of the ravine, for the horses would not be turned. In a steady stream, rapidly, never in a charging cluster which might have served as a means of shielding an advance of the outlaws on their enemy, the mustangs shot away into the open plain and left their masters without the means of transport!

What a howling they put up, then, like furious wild beasts. What a raging of oaths and execrations they poured out on Trainor. But he lay snug in his post. He was, in truth, like a small cork in a great bottle, and the powerful contents were held in check by his single gun, easily. Now that these fellows were dismounted, even if they were to escape from the valley at this moment, a good many of them would almost unquestionably be caught by the men who would soon be coming out from Alkali. Perhaps already Silver was in town, sounding the alarm to all good citizens and believers in the law.

Ben Trainor heard the shouted arguments, now and again, the raging, the groaning of these lost men. He heard them damn Christian bitterly. And then silence followed. They were evidently about to make another effort.

Presently he could make out what it was. He had already mentioned one of several rocks that projected near the top of the wall at the bottom of the box canyon and suggested that he would accept as a ransom for the rest the hanging of Christian and Yates. Now he saw a rope that mounted invisibly, slowly, toward one of those projections.

No doubt a rock that was attached to a light twine or cord had been thrown over the rock first, and now hands that were protected from view on the floor of the canyon were pulling up a rope. It was brought up carefully. A shuddering and awful hope came to Trainor that perhaps the outlaws had actually determined to take advantage of his offer. That rope, invisibly drawn, reached the top of a projecting drop and then fell off the end of it like a thin-bodied serpent, curling in the air.

Another try was made on another projection. This time, the curiously watching eye of Trainor enabled him to see the flinging of the rock, the small shadow showing dimly, in the moonlight, against the smooth of the cliff. He saw the rope begin to rise again, drawn by the invisible cord. And then he paid for the heedless manner in which he had exposed head and shoulder.

He had his rifle at the shoulder, pointed, ready for any target that might present itself as he looked out, when a single gun spoke, and a rifle bullet clanged on the barrel and butt of his weapon. It slashed through his upper arm and lodged behind his shoulder. He could feel it like a fist inside his flesh.

He lay flat on his face, for a moment, gripping his teeth to keep from groaning aloud in his misery. After that, he fell to work on the bandaging.

The blood was running out of him at a frightful rate. He got his shirt off with difficulty and cut it into rags that he tied together and then twisted and retwisted around his shoulder and the mangled flesh of the upper arm. For all the pressure that he put on, he was not able to stop the bleeding entirely. The drain continued steadily, though, of course, in a much diminished degree.

And the pain of the flesh, crushed together as it was by the binding grip of the bandage, sickened him. He looked up, feeling that the light of the moon had grown dimmer, and then he saw the dull and muddy color of the sunrise beginning in the sky.

Well, Silver was far off in Alkali, by this time, and perhaps already he was galloping on the road of the return. Let his coming be swift!

When Trainor ventured another glance, he saw that a doubled rope depended from the rock projection, near the top of the cliff—within arm's reach of the crest, in fact. And then, grasping the two ropes and pulling himself up with the ape-like speed of a sailor in rigging, appeared Blacky. He was easily known, even in that baffling light of the moon and the dawn, by the build of his body and the bandage around his head. And there was something gallant in this desperate attempt of his that stopped the heart of Trainor.

There was no time for admiration, however. The rifle fire was showering about him again, more rapidly than ever. It was at the risk of his own life that he exposed the tip of his head, took quick aim, and fired.

He saw Blacky droop, and hang by one hand like a wounded monkey, so he ducked back under the rock with a shudder of disgust and remorse.

A shout startled him. He looked again, and saw that Blacky, wounded or not, had resumed his climbing, and was now standing on the rock projection and actually reaching for the rim of the cliff.

Again Trainor fired. He missed, and Blacky pulled himself right up on the edge of the rock as Trainor tried with a third bullet.

He saw Blacky twist into a knot and roll over the verge of the height, then drop down, his heavy body spinning over and over.

Very distinctly, Trainor heard the awful impact of the body against the ground. It sickened him, it weakened him through every nerve. He lay flat once more, thankful that the grisly business was ended. They would surely give over their efforts now and accept the fate that waited for them.

In fact, a dead silence settled over the ravine and continued for so long that Trainor grew suspicious and looked out again. A swishing of bullets through the sand about him proved that the men of Christian were on the alert. But the ropes dangled naked from the cliff.

There was this advantage—that he could see the upper portion of the ropes without exposing himself a great deal. So he kept his glance from time to time fixed on them, while the moon sank in the west, and the dawn turned red, and suddenly the dazzling eye of the sun was shining down upon him.

The warmth of it soaked like hot water into the increasing agony of his wound. Shooting, if he had to do any, would be more difficult, now, because the arm was half numb from the pull of the bandages and the pain of the flesh.

The sun climbed higher in that mortal silence. And why did not Silver appear? Yet when Trainor turned his head, again and again, he saw no sign of a dust cloud across the broad face of the desert.

At last, it seemed to him that the ropes were jerking a little. When he ventured a glance, it was to see a coatless, bootless man climbing up the face of the rock on the ropes. His long hair blew out in the wind. The power in those long arms and the broad shoulders made Trainor think of Jim Silver—and by that token he knew that it was Barry Christian!

Christian, at last, for a target! And perhaps it would be for Silver's rifle, in the hands of another, to end the long trail of Barry Christian!

Trainor drew his bead. It was not easy, because Christian, as he climbed, was swinging his body violently, and this caused him to sway in strong, irregular pulsations from side to side. He had a rifle strapped at his back, and the barrel of the gun flashed in the sun.

Trainor fired at that wavering image.

The report of his gun brought a crashing volley from both sides of the valley, close to the mouth of the ravine. In order to center their shots and aim with a better chance, the men of Christian were exposing themselves recklessly, standing up from their rock screens. They were sheltering their leader, but they were fighting for their own lives.

A bullet slicked across the side of Trainor's head. It was a mere graze. It felt as though a sharp edge of ice had been whipped across the scalp. Then the blood rushed out.

He fired again, and again he knew that he had missed that dangling, swinging target!

Now Christian reached and pulled up on the projecting rock. The time had come when he would have to straighten and haul himself up to the edge of the cliff, and this was the chance of Trainor to place a careful shot in the target.

So he waited, tense, calm, sure of himself, only wishing that the ghastly throbbing in his right arm would ease for the important instant. He took his aim as Christian rose on the rock. He began to squeeze with his whole hand.

And then Christian leaped like a stag, right out of the intended path of the bullet. For he had gripped the verge of the cliff with one hand, and then sprung up as a man would do in vaulting a fence. Trainor fired, cursing his luck at the very instant that he pressed the trigger, and Christian rolled—untouched, he knew—into safety over the lip of the rock.

A babel of mad rejoicing rose out of the ravine, at that. What a cheering and what a mighty yelling went up in honor of a great leader!

For, of course, the battle was won now. Christian had merely to creep out to a vantage point high up on either side of the entrance to the ravine, and from that place he could shoot down at an angle that would make the rocks of Trainor a useless shelter for his body.

But Trainor could not stand up and flee. The watchers inside the valley would riddle him instantly with bullets. There was nothing for him to do but lie there and wait for the coming stroke of agony and death.

There were no calm thoughts, there was no remorse in his mind. There was only a savage rage because the great plan was balked, in this fashion, at the very last moment.

Eagerly he scanned the upper ridges of the rocks. It

might be that Barry Christian would expose himself a trifle when making his shot, and in that case—

The minutes grew. An impatient shouting began in the valley.

"Barry! Hey, Christian! Come to life! Come to life! Do something! I can hear them coming now!"

Yes, it was true. A beating of hoofs sounded softly in the ears of Trainor. He turned his head, and out of a growing cloud of dust, he saw riders coming; he saw the golden flash of the great stallion, running far in the lead.

And Christian?

Why, from the height he had seen the coming danger, and instead of staying to liberate his imprisoned men by firing a single bullet into the man who had blocked the way to freedom, he had simply sped away to give himself a better start.

CHAPTER XXV

A Reformed Town

THERE might have been a battle to the death, of course. Or at least the outlaws might have waited until the enemy had mounted the rim rock that overlooked the ravine, and so made resistance useless. But the desertion of Christian seemed to take the heart away from the other men. They simply threw up their hands and walked out to be tied hand to hand by the directions, not of Jim Silver, but of the deputy sheriff.

Yes, he was there to glory in the work to which so long he had not dared to put his hand. He was there to greet by name and special insult all of the men from the ravine, except one.

It was after the others had come out that a single shot was heard from the canyon.

"That's Yates," said Perry. "He'd never live to be tried. He'd rather go out this way than be shamed!"

They found Yates, in fact, sitting against a rock and looking east at the blazing sun with open, dead eyes. He had shot himself through the temple. As the gun fell to the sand, his hands had dropped folded into his lap. He seemed to be smiling in contemplation of another world. He was buried beside Blacky.

Jim Silver was not there for the funeral ceremonies, brief as they were. When he learned that the great prize had actually escaped from the canyon, he had thrown up his long arms with a cry that tore the soul of poor Trainor with remorse. Then, without a word, he had rushed with Parade and Frosty in the pursuit.

But the rest of the party went slowly back across the desert toward Alkali, and the whole town came out to meet them.

It was a wonderful thing to Ben Trainor to see that greeting! He had thought that in the whole of the town there was hardly a single man that really cared about law and order. Now it appeared that everyone, nearly, had been terrorized, and now that the terror had been removed, there was a great wave of rejoicing.

They made a hero out of Trainor in spite of himself. They pointed him out to one another. Except for his wounds, they would have ridden him through the streets on their shoulders. They had to content themselves with striding beside his horse and cheering themselves hoarse.

So Trainor came past the Golden Hope.

It was a wreck. Axes and hammers were battering it to pieces. The gambling machines were being thrown out into the street, at that moment, under the supervision of a fat man, who spoke with an authority that was obeyed by everyone. That was Doctor Wells.

He came hastily to Trainor. From the suffocating strain of the sand storm he had quite recovered. He was only a little pale, and the sweat of labor ran down his face, because he had organized the smashing of the Golden Hope. There was already a murmur running through the place that a reformed town needed a reformed man for mayor, and that Wells should be the one for the job.

He gripped the hand of Trainor and shouted:

"Everything's all right! Clive's asleep like a baby. He's too tough to be more than dented by what he's been through. The girl's happy as a queen, and I'm happy as a king. It's all owing to you, Ben! The town knows it. I know it. More power to you, lad!"

Then the crowd poured on, carrying Ben Trainor with it.

Wells came after him to dress his wounds. But before Ben Trainor would let his hurts be touched, he looked in for a glance at Clive, in the hotel room where he lay, and saw him smiling in his sleep, while Nell sat beside him, brooding, happy forever.

The loss of blood hurt Ben Trainor almost more than the tearing of his flesh by the twisting bullet. He lay in a semi-stupor for two days and nights; after that, he began to recover rapidly.

When townsmen representative of the newly organized vigilance committee came to ask what they could do for him, he requested only one thing—freedom for Perry. It was granted at once, and Perry came to see him before leaving town—under escort.

Big and rangy, brown-faced, with a careless blue eye, Perry sat beside Trainor for a long time.

He said, smiling: "I'm through, Trainor. I thought I was tough enough to hit the high spots with the wildest hombres on earth. But all I turned out to be was a mama's boy that was playing hookey. Now I'm going back to the range and punch cows. You'll be hearing from me one of these days."

Perry was not the only visitor who came to see Trainor as he lay in the sick bed. Others dropped in, from time to time, and the most persistent were the reporters who were wanting to make him famous. Nell came, too, several times a day, with reports about the progress of Clive, and how the mine was being opened, offering a tide of wealth that increased the more the vein was developed. She and Clive had declared a third interest in favor of Ben.

"You ought to have half, at least," said the girl, "but we knew that you wouldn't take it."

She was almost stunned with happiness. The marriage was to take place as soon as Clive was pronounced fit and well by the doctor.

The doctor himself was often with Ben Trainor, looking pale and nervous, but firm to that temperance pledge which he had made in the silence of that moonlight night under Mount Baldy.

It was on the fourth day that the dance hall girl, Dolly, appeared. Trainor hardly recognized her. The make-up was gone from her face. She wore a sober gray street dress and a gray hat, and she sat on the side of the bed and looked Trainor over with a smile.

"The game kids are the ones that bring home the bacon," she said.

"Where's all the decoration, Dolly?" Trainor asked her.

She rubbed the tips of her fingers over her face, letting the touch linger around her eyes.

"Aw, what's the use of the bother?" asked Dolly. "I'm going home and cut out the rough stuff. I'm sick of everything. You made me sick of everything."

"You're in mourning, Dolly," he told her. "Who for or what for?"

"For Doc Yates," she answered him frankly.

"Yates!" he exclaimed.

"Yeah," said Dolly. "He was a big crook. I always knew that. But I loved him. Not so much that I'm going to fade away, but enough so's I don't want to put on the war paint as long as that crook isn't around to see it."

"Girls are funny," said Ben Trainor, with a sigh and a shake of his head.

"Yeah, and you don't know how funny we are," said Dolly. "Girls and towns are funny. Look at Alkali. They're going to plant trees in the streets, and have a park, and everything. Look what you did to us, Ben!"

"I didn't do it," said Trainor. "What a sick mess I would have made of everything, if Jim Silver hadn't dropped in at the right time."

"Aw, sure. There's Silver, of course, but he doesn't count," said the girl. "He's not human. He's not like the rest of us. He's the sort of thing you pray for, and it comes true once in your life."

News of Silver, there was none, or of how his chase after Christian had progressed. Then, one night Trainor heard a light scratching sound at the door of his room. The door was opened, because of the heat, and he saw the gigantic head of Frosty framed against the black of the hall, with red, lolling tongue, and bright green eyes. Behind him loomed Silver, who entered with a long, noiseless stride.

He sat down and took the hand of Trainor and held it for a long time.

Silver was thin. There were great hollows under his eyes; his cheek bones stood out. The hunger of an unfilled yearning was still straining the lines about his eyes. He had been through a most apparent hell.

"Ah, Jim, you missed him!" said Trainor.

"I missed him," said Silver, nodding. "How are you, old son?"

"I'm sick, thinking about the way I let Christian get away. The right arm was pretty numb. And then—Christian went up that rope like a flying snipe. I never saw anything like it. I missed him three times, I guess!"

Silver said: "Forget about it. One day I'll meet him. It's not going to be with other people around, I imagine. There'll be nothing to stop us. There won't be weapons, either. It'll be bare hands, I suppose. And then—a finish —maybe for both of us."

He spoke dreamily. But long, long afterwards Trainor was to remember those words.

"Jim," he said, "what do you get out of all this? You split my share in the mine, will you? It's rich as sin. There's too much loot in it for just the three of us!"

Silver smiled at him.

"Money doesn't stick to me," he said. "And gold is a mighty heavy weight to carry on the sort of a trail I have to ride. Maybe I'll meet you on that trail some time, Ben. That is, if you ever go broke!"

He laughed, stood an instant in the doorway, smiling back at Trainor, and then was gone, with the gray wolf at his heels.